Third Wheel

Elite Escorts 2

Lynn Burke

Third Wheel

As Elite Escort's most sought-after third wheel, I'm responsible for fulfilling clients' fantasies of bringing another man into the mix for a night of debauchery.

But I've grown bored with my night job and want more.

Jessica Lindy's friend hires EE to take her out and show her a good time. Although single dates aren't my usual assignments, I agree to fulfill the task. Jessica steals my breath at first sight, and before our evening ends, I plan on worshiping at her feet for the rest of our lives.

But she's jaded. A single mom with no time or energy to entertain dreams of happily ever after.

Her heart isn't available thanks to her ex-husband, who she helped put behind bars, and constant fear over his vow of revenge keeps her from enjoying life.

When nightmares become a reality, she and her daughter end up in grave danger.

Can I convince Jessica I'm more than just a professional third wheel, or will the man intent on payback take her from me before I get the chance?

Chapter 1

Reid

Same as every time they requested my presence for the night, Mrs. Kimball answered the door to my quiet rap. A sheer, white nightgown fell mid-thigh over her curvy body, offering me an eyeful of large, dark nipples and the trimmed patch of hair between her thighs.

"Reid." She breathed my name, arousal already coating her voice.

"Mrs. Kimball," I greeted. "New nightie?"

"Of course." The slight lines around her eyes crinkled with her smile I couldn't help but return. It was no secret her husband spoiled her rotten.

She stepped back to allow me entrance to the hotel suite I'd been visiting every other Friday the previous four months since signing on with Elite Escorts in January.

I stepped past her and breathed in the scent of subtle yet expensive perfume I would be washing off my body before our session's end.

I sold myself for sex. Or, rather, Micah, one of my closest friends and the owner of Elite Escorts hired me to satisfy the customers whose requests fit my profile. Tall, dark, and handsome, I was a professional who knew how to fulfill client's fantasies of having a second man on hand for a night of debauchery.

Pleasuring the women who paid for me was easy enjoyable money, every time.

Why I'd fought Micah's begging to pimp me out for his company for over a year, I didn't know. It had taken a whirlwind romance and a broken heart to open my eyes to the fact fucking around would always be better than attempting something long-term.

I would never fall in love again.

To each their own, but I would never personally offer to satisfying a lover's fantasy about sharing her with another man. And I sure as fuck would never have given her a diamond ring on Christmas morning after knowing her for two months only to have her keep the damn thing when she left me on New Year's for the guy we'd invited into our bed.

A muscle in my jaw ticked at the thought of my ex, but at least the lingering pain in my chest no longer felt like someone gouged me with a serrated knife.

Because of Tara, I'd become one of Elite Escort's most requested third wheels, a man who knew his place in others' beds and had zero interest in getting emotionally involved with clients.

I followed Mrs. Kimball into the sunken sitting area where her husband lounged butt naked on the white leather couch, a tumbler of scotch in his grasp.

A good twenty or so years older than me, Mr. Kimball kept himself in good shape. He was tanned, still ripped, and had a full head of hair with silver at the temples. And like me, he had no need of little blue pills.

The older man always gave me a run for the money with his wife moaning between us, but while he had stamina, I bounced back ten times faster. He often enjoyed watching the second go-round his wife always begged for while sipping on another scotch.

"Mr. Sullivan," he said, gesturing to the chair across from him, gracious as always. "My wife has been panting for you all week."

"Is that a fact?" I quirked a brow and sat while studying the quiet woman who stood between us.

Cheeks flushed and pulse already thrumming in her neck, she lowered her head, hands clasped in front of her. She was perfectly submissive and sweet. Not my type personality-wise, but her body made getting hard easy.

"Mmm." Mr. Kimball swallowed some of his liquor. "That's a fact."

I loosened my tie before settling back into the leather seat, ready to move things along. "On your knees, Buttercup."

Mrs. Kimball hardly resembled the little yellow flower I'd have preferred, but that was the pet name I'd been supplied with the first time I'd been hired to play with them. The dark eyes and hair running in waves over her tightly furled nipples suggested an Italian or Greek heritage.

She was gorgeous but easy for me to keep at emotional arm's length. It was sassy and independent blondes alone who tended to capture my focus and tempt my mind beyond sex.

She sauntered closer, all swaying hips and sensual curves I could appreciate.

The thought of her warm, talented mouth sucking on my dick roused life in my groin, and I rested my forearms on the chair's armrests.

Pupils already blown, she sank to her knees between my

thighs and unbuckled my belt. Her lips parted, breaths coming in shallow gasps as though she already hovered on the edge of climaxing.

I didn't need to glance over at her husband to see what he thought of his cock-hungry wife getting on her knees for another man. He gave and gave without hesitation because of his love for her.

Same as I'd done with Tara.

A hiss left my mouth as Mrs. Kimball's hand slid into my slacks and grasped my length. All thoughts of my ex fled as the dark-haired beauty leaned closer, her focus on the swollen head of my dick. Her warm, wet mouth closed around me, and I released a groan, grabbing a handful of her lush locks.

Mr. Kimball let out a quiet curse, but no trace of jealousy laced his tone. Nothing pleased him more than gifting his wife with what she craved.

Twice a month, it was an abundance of dick.

Her teeth scraped along my length with the perfect amount of sting, her smooth hand reaching deeper inside my pants to cup my balls and pull a rumbled murmur of approval from me.

She bobbed over my length, slurping and sucking, gagging and moaning.

"So good, Buttercup." I gave her the praise that always made her skin shiver with goosebumps. "Your mouth feels amazing."

She doubled her efforts to suck cum from me, quickly drawing my balls up tight. Humming her pleasure, she took me deep and swallowed, her throat tightening around my glans.

"Christ, woman." I tightened my fist in her hair and

yanked her off me since she would want me in her other two holes and I didn't have three loads in me.

She let go with a pop, her lips glistening with saliva and the pre-cum she had effortlessly enticed up my shaft. Large, doe-like eyes peered up at me, the brown of her irises eaten by her swollen pupils.

"Your husband looks a little lonely." I forced her head around toward him while tugging down on my balls. "Go suck his cock but keep that gorgeous backside on display for me."

She did as told, crawling across the plush rug between us men, her nightgown rising above her round ass. A blue-jeweled plug peeked from between her cheeks, and wetness coated her pussy and upper thighs.

I tugged my tie off and started on my shirt's buttons while Mrs. Kimball's head nestled between her husband's thighs, ass high just like I'd commanded. He swigged his scotch, face impassive, seeming unmoved as he watched her lick up the back of his dick.

He'd already made his requests for the evening via Micah, so I set about to please our customers.

"You can do better than that, Buttercup," I told Mrs. Kimball, standing to shove down my slacks. One yank freed my belt, and I dropped the pants to the floor, folding the leather strip in half. "Swallow him down and arch your back for me."

Her husband's gaze rose to me as I drew near.

I quirked an eyebrow just to double check.

He nodded, impassive as always, but heat in his eyes betrayed his arousal.

While I didn't enjoy dishing out pain, I gave the man what he wanted—what his wife had requested—with a half-hearted downward swipe. The crack of leather on skin caused them both to flinch.

A shudder rippled down her body, and she moaned around her husband's cock, her spine bowing even deeper.

"Like that do you?" I asked, my cock jerking as she groaned her agreement. Two more quick swats and cherry red stripes rose along her golden skin.

A sheen of sweat beaded on Mr. Kimball's brow, and he clenched his jaw. He sat still like a fucking pro though as his wife worked him over and I continued to rain down somewhat gentle lashes over her backside and thighs.

She squirmed and whimpered, choking herself on her husband's cock.

"Fuck." Mr. Kimball's gaze flickered up to me, the haze of lust in his pale eyes begging me to end his torment.

Mr. Kimball didn't have a submissive bone in his body, but he loved giving me control over them—because his wife asked him for it.

"Enough," I stated quietly while sliding my shirt from my shoulders but retaining my grip on my belt.

A slow hissed exhale left Mr. Kimball as his wife backed off, rocking onto her heels.

"Strip, Buttercup," I told her.

Mr. Kimball stared at her like a man possessed, longing and something beyond mere need for release in his steady gaze.

A flame of jealousy licked at my chest as her nightie fluttered to the floor.

Once upon a time, I had wanted what they shared—passion, honesty, and *commitment*...

"Straddle him but face me," I said, moving toward the couple, forcing my focus on earning my money. "Sit on his cock. Take him balls deep in that soaked pussy of yours."

Gaze on my jutting hard-on, Mrs. Kimball started to lower, teeth biting into her lip.

Mr. Kimball grabbed hold of her flared hips and slammed her down onto him.

Both of their groans ricocheted through me, and I grasped my dick, pulling upward until a bead of pre-cum welled at my slit.

Her husband spread their thighs and moved her up and down over his shaft, making her full tits bounce with each thrust, but she didn't remove her focus from my cock.

Knowing she wanted a taste, I dabbed at the wetness with my fingertip and stepped closer, holding out my hand. "Lick."

She eagerly leaned forward, hands on her husband's knees, her tongue flicking over the sticky pad of my finger.

"More," she whispered.

Shaking my head, I narrowed my gaze, the sight of them fucking mere feet away heating my blood. "You don't deserve more."

She pouted, but I ignored her pleading eyes and returned to stroking myself with one hand, the other still loosely holding the folded leather at my side. "Mr. Kimball told me you've been a naughty girl this week."

Her mouth opened but snapped shut as I ran my belt along her cheek and down her neck to her bouncing breasts. Eyes closing, she moaned over the wet sucking noises of her husband's thrusts into her sopping pussy.

I lightly flicked the leather against one bare breast then the other.

"Oh, God." She groaned and leaned against her husband's chest, back arching as though asking for another lash.

Eyes closed, Mr. Kimball continued fucking up into her,

lips in a grim line as though fighting off the tightness of his balls hugging the base of his dick.

I guessed me giving his wife pain turned him the fuck on. Couldn't have him blowing too soon though.

Dropping the belt, I squatted between their splayed thighs, grasping hold of hers. "No coming until I say so."

Mr. Kimball's thrusts slowed, and I latched my mouth onto his wife's clit, the scent of her musky arousal flooding my nose and filling my lungs.

She let out a loud whimper, hips bucking toward me as I suckled.

Mr. Kimball released his hold on her hips, arms wrapping around her core to still her movements. The slow gyrations of his hips and my lips and tongue had her panting and squirming in a matter of seconds.

"I'm going to come." She gasped, but I pulled back and swatted her clit.

A shriek tore from her lips, and she jerked atop her husband's cock.

"P-please." Her heated, hazed eyes lifted to meet mine.

I backed away and stood. "On the floor, Mr. Kimball. Your sweet wife is going to ride you like it's her last day on earth."

They both complied, Mr. Kimball stretching out on the plush rug, abs tight, soaked cock pulsing. The brief respite allowed him to draw a few breaths and eased the furrow between his eyebrows.

He reached for her as I retrieved the condom and packet of lube from my pants pocket.

His wife impaled herself without hesitation, her moan mixing in my ears with his curse.

Mrs. Kimball's jeweled ass jiggled as she attempted to

make amends for being a brat that week. By her husband's groans, I knew she did a good job.

I sheathed myself and knelt behind them, gaze latched on her pink folds sucking on his thick girth. Before night's end, I would feel the same sensations as he did—but first things first.

"Do you think she's earned her reward, Mr. Kimball?" I asked, squirting lube onto my hand and slicking up my cock.

"Yes." He ground out the word, and I pressed a palm to his wife's back to urge her forward over his chest.

"Lay still for me, so I can see how ready you are to take my dick." I grasped the end of the butt plug and teased her a bit, working it around, in and out.

She whimpered but relaxed like I'd told her to.

"Such a good girl," I crooned a few minutes later, sliding the plug free and grasping her hips.

I'd learned the first time with the couple that the wife preferred a brutal ass fucking rather than slow and easy, so I pressed the tip of my dick to her slack hole.

"Breathe, Buttercup." I slammed into her tight ass, balls deep.

She cried out and tried to move, but I held her in a vise grip. "Your pleasure belongs to us, Mrs. Kimball."

I nodded at her husband, and on his thrust, I backed off, leaving only my swollen tip inside her tight ring. I plunged back in, Mr. Kimball retreating in perfect harmony with my movement.

We fucked her hard and fast, heavy breaths, groans, and the wet smacking of skin the only noise in the hotel room.

Mr. Kimball's jaw clenched, sweat dripping down his temples. The closing of his eyes let me know he neared his end.

I slapped both of his wife's ass cheeks to take my mind

off my seized-up balls begging to explode. One more slap and I reached my limit too.

"You have permission to come." The words rasped from my throat, and Mrs. Kimball's guttural scream brought a satisfied smirk to my lips and a massive explosion of cum into the condom.

JE

Showered and redressed two hours later, I crept past the open bedroom door to let myself out as I always did once the Kimballs finished with me for the night.

They lay entwined beneath a thin sheet, her head on his chest and lips parted in satiated sleep.

Thank you, Mr. Kimball mouthed at me.

I dipped my head.

He sighed and closed his eyes, his arms wrapping around his wife, a smile finally relaxing his features.

A few minutes later, I pulled out of the hotel's parking garage and into Boston's downtown, rain splattering over my truck.

Discontentment poured over me like rivulets of water, not easily swiped away by windshield wipers.

For four months, I'd been having a shit load of sex in every way and every place imaginable. I'd lost count of how many orifices my sheathed cock had become well acquainted with minus the hassle of feelings and emotional entanglement.

Living every man's dream, I should have been riding on the top of the world.

I'm fucking empty.

The thought pinged between my ears louder than the raindrops on the metal around me.

Seeing the Kimballs lying together in sated contentment, sharing a bond I had hoped to experience once upon a time, twisted my stomach up tight.

I had thought I'd found a woman like Mrs. Kimball, one who adored her partner's love language of giving, but the recipient of my heart's desire had proven to be a selfish bitch.

She'd taken and taken, leaving me desolate in the end.

I heaved a breath as the murkiness of the Sumner Tunnel surrounded me, cutting off the vigorous rain.

Shattered promises of early morning cuddles and happily ever afters only made the shadows surrounding my truck darker, intensifying my sense of loss. Dissatisfaction over being nothing more than a third wheel swelled inside me, but I wouldn't allow myself another option.

True love and contentment would never appear like a beckoning light on the horizon.

Even if my broken heart longed for it.

Chapter 2

Jessica

Praying the transferred call was for a sale, I put on my headset and forced a smile while clicking on the insurance quote shortcut on my work computer's screen.

"This is Jessica Lindy," I said, my voice brightened only by choice. "How can I help you today?"

"Sorry to bother you at work, Jessie—"

I heaved an exhale, my lips flatlining at the voice of my daughter's daycare owner.

"—but Cassie is running a high fever, and someone needs to come pick her up."

My stomach tightened, worry overshadowing my disappointment in not having the opportunity to earn a little extra cash that week for signing up a new customer.

"I'll be there as soon as I can." I disconnected the call and pulled off my headset. "This is when having a family close by would be a huge help," I mumbled to myself, swiveling around in my chair to face the cubicle behind me.

Christine, Gemberling Insurance's future owner and my immediate boss, sat against the building's back wall where she could oversee the main room. Her father, the business owner, had offered her one of the glass-enclosed offices to my right, but Christine liked to keep an eye on her "flock" as she called the four agents working for them.

I knew the truth about my friend though. She loved being in the thick of the action, able to hear whatever gossip made its round on a daily basis.

I caught her attention over the counter hiding her desk from view and waited for her call to end.

While she discussed a claim with one of the adjusters, I considered the pickle I found myself in. As a single mom who didn't have much family to speak of let alone get along with, I once more faced having to leave work without pay to care for my child.

I would never regret Cassie, but I sure as hell wished I could take back the choice of getting tangled up with her father.

"What's up, Jessie?" Christine asked, pulling her headset off her hair. Strands of flaming red entangled in the earpiece, but she yanked it free with a scowl. "Fucking piece of shit. We seriously need new ones."

I didn't argue, seeing as how my own straw-colored hair often got caught in my headset. "Cassie is running a fever again."

"Damnit." Christine tossed down her pen, but I knew her annoyance wasn't over my words. She was well aware of my predicament—my financial and family status. "You don't have any sick or personal days left."

"I know." I bit the inside of my lip.

"If Dad had retired last year like he was supposed to, I would be the boss and could help you out."

My heart sank at the prospect to a cut, much-needed

paycheck like I'd expected, but at least Christine would keep him from firing me. "I understand."

She glanced up at the clock over the front door. "It's close enough to your lunch break. I'll make sure you get a half day's pay at least."

Tears stung my eyelids, and I swallowed hard. "Thanks."

Compassion softened her green-eyed gaze. "Go get your little bossy-boo and give her some snuggles. Hopefully, she's feeling better by Monday so you won't have to miss any more work."

Still choked up, I nodded.

"And even if she isn't, I don't want you worrying yourself sick. You do enough of that already. Just take care of her. Take care of yourself. Your job will be here and waiting when you're able to get back, okay?"

I relayed a shuddered exhale, my wobbly smile real for a change. "I will."

"You're our most hard-working employee and one hell of a mom, Jessie," she told me. "Cassie is lucky to have you."

Her words tightened my throat even more—especially since I knew how much the loss of her own mom had affected her.

"Thanks," I whispered and spun around in my chair to shut down my computer and gather my things before I burst into tears.

The earlier Massachusetts's cold spring morning had required a heavy coat when the office had opened at eight, but I draped it over my arm when stepping out into the bright sunshine. The glowing orb heating the air celebrated in opposition to the status of my life. The sky should have hung overcast. Threatening rain. Thunder rumbling and grumbling in dissatisfaction of withholding a shower of rain —tears.

Biting them back had become a daily occurrence, but once I burrowed beneath my covers at night where I could finally let my guard down, I allowed them to flow.

My stinging eyes threatened nonstop even after I slouched in my car. My twelve-year-old Camry hesitated when I turned the key, the engine spitting and sputtering.

"Come on, you piece of shit," I whispered through my clogged throat. "Be good to me. Please."

Another try and the damn thing came to life.

Heaving a huge exhale, I shifted and left my saving grace of a job behind in the rearview mirror. My stomach refused to unclench from worry over Cassie and my finances as I pulled onto the highway and headed north on Route 1.

Unsure of what sat in the medicine cabinet in my apartment beyond a little children's pain reliever, I decided I had better stop for more in case Cassie ended up being sick for a few days like she usually did when running a random fever. The drugstore came into view ahead, and I pulled over, hating how I had to count and keep a tight rein on every penny I earned.

Generic grape chewables in hand, I headed toward the front. The local newspaper on a rack by the cashier caught my eye, and I halted, scanning the headline.

Attempted Prison Break.

I shifted my gaze to the pictures of the two convicts, their black and white mugs taking up most of the front page. Heart thudding in my chest, I grabbed a copy to make sure my eyes didn't deceive me.

Devon.

Tremors ripped through me, and I dragged my focus off

dark eyes that still haunted my nightmares to the article above his picture.

An attempted escape foiled by a fellow inmate, it read.

"Thank God." The ragged whisper tore from my throat as other curses flitted through my head. I put the paper back on the rack and turned from the visual reminder of my past to set the medicine on the counter.

My fingers shook as I handed over payment, my mind a buzz of flitting thoughts, my emotions tumbling over one another.

Devon, my ex-husband, had been found guilty of bank robbery three years earlier and had gotten locked behind bars—thanks to me.

We'd been together for two rocky years prior to that, the last of which I'd spent trying to help him break his newly-found addiction to drugs. I'd stayed with him in the hopes of healing the only man who had ever claimed to love me.

Broke and needing a fix, he and his buddy had robbed a bank and would have gotten away with it if I hadn't recognized his face on the fuzzy security picture the local news had shown a day later when asking for help in locating the two men.

By that time, I had been trapped in a prison of my own making, and I didn't know how to escape. I'd felt enough of Devon's barbed words and the occasional fists that I'd decided turning him in would help my husband get clean and possibly save my life.

A couple of weeks after Devon's arrest, I'd found out I was pregnant and decided to write him with the news regardless of his hatred of me for betraying him.

He'd scrawled a reply, a few half-illegible words about my being a whore and that he wasn't the father of the bastard in my belly. The final line about getting back at me for what I'd done to him had choked the air from my lungs, prompting me to uproot and move out of town the day after his trial ended with him getting locked up.

Cassie had become my reason for living. My mini-me filled my life with joy even if I had ended up like I said I never would...just like my mom. Single and trying to raise a kid on my own. Throw in a jaded heart, and I reminded myself of her too much for comfort. Barely scraping by on a small paycheck and having to cut my hours short...

Pull up your big girl panties.

Swallowing yet another threat of tears, I gritted my teeth and attempted to start my car. The damn thing gave me its usual hesitation and complaints of tiredness, muttering with choked exhaust coughs about how much it wanted to end up as a pile of scrap metal in a junkyard somewhere.

"Start already!" I barked, my eyes hazed over.

Maybe someday I would catch a break. Maybe win the lottery. Maybe even find a way to replenish my energy since I struggled like hell on my own to provide for my child even though I was determined to do so.

Devon had created a wreck in his wake, and like my car, I struggled to move through life without difficulty.

Fears of failure enticed me to hit the snooze on my alarm every morning.

Expecting the worst to happen promised a daily throb between my ears.

Worries kept me up at night.

And trust the memory of him and his threats to slink along into my dreams while I slept.

He had called me weak enough times while we'd been together that I'd realized the truth of my sorry existence. He'd claimed I'd been lucky to have him, how I couldn't possibly ever make it on my own. But goddamnit, I had a child to provide for, and I would do so even if it took me to an early grave.

Choking on a sob, I rested my forehead on my steering wheel. "Please start," I whispered, needing to escape the clouds settling over my shoulders regardless of the sun warming my face through the windshield. "Please."

The engine turned over, and I sat back, blinking away tears.

I *would* make it on my own. I *had* to.

Cassie deserved so much more than I'd missed out on in life. One day, I hoped she would find someone to love her as much as I did, but they would have to come in the form of her own partner.

I wouldn't ever be able to trust another man enough to invite him into our lives.

Chapter 3

Reid

"Missed you Saturday night," I grumbled at Blake as I followed him into the trailer-office parked on the jobsite of the new high school his company had been hired to build.

The two windows opposite each other propped open, allowing the cool spring breeze to air out the small area where he and I sat every morning to go over the progress while downing our coffee.

"That's what, now? Three?" I asked. "Four guy's nights in a row you've skipped out on?"

"Wren and I had plans," my best friend and daytime employer explained while sitting and rolling the chair's wheels to draw closer to his desk.

I pressed my lips tight and settled into the folding metal chair across from him, envy growing inside me like it always did whenever he mentioned his girlfriend.

We had shared her the first time she allowed him into her bed, but that had ended up being a one-and-done. She'd finally agreed to go out with him a few weeks later, and he got all possessive and shit.

"How's Wren doing with finals coming up?" I asked since I *did* like the girl who'd stolen his heart.

"Stressed." Blake sipped his coffee, eyeing the plans haphazardly pinned down atop his desk. "I was helping her study all weekend."

"You couldn't take a break?" I pushed, sounding like a petulant brat, but I couldn't help it. I missed my best friend.

"Oh, we took plenty of breaks." He grinned, and I flipped him the bird.

"Well, tell her I said good luck and that your ass belongs to me for a whole weekend once she graduates next month."

"She doesn't share."

"Fuck off," I muttered.

Chuckling, he took another swallow of his coffee and sat back in his chair. "What's the fuck crawled up your ass and died? You're grumpy as shit."

"Told you, man," I replied, stretching out my legs to relax. "Guy's night isn't the same, and you know I'm not a fan of change."

It used to be him, Colton, Micah, and I, faithful as fuck every Wednesday or Friday night. Then Colton had gotten all tangled up with a married couple who adored the fuck out of him, and Blake had weaseled his way into Wren's heart.

I went to work for Micah which gobbled up most of my Fridays, so we'd ended switching to Saturdays when our schedules allowed. Jarod, another of his Elites, had started to join us for beers and burgers if he wasn't on the clock too.

"That shit with Tara bothering you again?" Blake asked.

I scowled, hating how he studied my face, his dark blue eyes full of concern. He'd been the one to go ring shopping with me the week before Christmas when I'd planned to propose to Tara.

She'd said yes. We'd fucked beside a tree decorated with twinkling lights.

Then six days later—

"Fuck." Groaning, I rubbed a hand over my face, weary as hell and wanting to rid my mind of that woman. "Getting dumped like that...yeah." I blew out a heavy exhale and slouched. "Messed with my head."

"How's the escort business going?"

"Good. Easy pussy. Even easier money." I shrugged. "What's not to love?"

"The lack of intimacy," Blake tossed out.

I narrowed my gaze, glaring at him across his desk. It sucked I felt as though I...*lacked*, that I worked a fuck ton of hours every week in order to escape the loneliness that clung to me.

"Think you'll ever try again?" Blake asked since he'd known me since childhood and that I wanted a family and a marriage like my parents shared. And after watching him fall head over heels for Wren the summer before, my envious heart had been easy pickings for Tara at the Halloween party where we'd met.

"I'm happy as-is, thank you very fucking much," I muttered.

"Liar."

No woman would get under my skin again and take advantage of my giving nature. Women like Mrs. Kimball were rare as unicorns, and I'd stopped dreaming of finding one of my own.

"Better to be alone than risk living through that kind of pain a second time," I stated quietly what I'd been telling myself for four months. Once had definitely been enough. "Where are we at?" I asked, tipping my chin toward the papers on his desk.

"Right on schedule," Blake replied, allowing me to change the subject. He shifted the plans in front of him around, scanning over the top page and filling me in on the prior week's accomplishments and what the next couple of days looked like.

A few minutes later, my cell dinged, and I pulled it from my back pocket to find my siblings' group chat had a new message.

Baby Sister One: **Guess what!**

Grinning, I went with the reply I'd been tossing back at her since childhood. **Chicken butt.**

Baby Sister Two: **Why guess? You're just going to brag about your latest triumph anyway.**

Baby Sister Three: **Need coffee. Brain no work this early.**

Chuckling, I watched the blinking dots while waiting for the oldest of my three younger siblings to drop her news.

Baby Sister One: **I'm pregnant again!**

Her message included a shit ton of heart-eyed emojis and happy faces.

"Holy fuck," I murmured, shaking my head. She'd had three kids in three years...the fuck was she thinking having a fourth already? "That husband of yours needs to keep his dick to himself," I snorted while typing out my congratulations.

"What's up?" Blake asked.

I muted my cell and shoved it back into my pocket, hating that sense of missing out on shit as present as ever in my mind. "Margo is pregnant."

"*Already?*" He barked out a laugh. "Are you *shitting* me?"

"Nope."

"Was this one planned?"

I shrugged. "She's definitely happy about it if those twelve emojis she included in her announcement are any clue."

"I knew all four of you Sullivan kids were hell-bent on having a baseball team each, but holy fuck. That'll be four kids in..."

"Four years," I filled in the blank, once more shaking my head. "My other sisters are trying for a second time too already."

"They just had a double wedding three years ago! What the fuck is the rush to pop out even more kids?"

I couldn't put an answer into words, but I understood their desire. Our parents had an incredible marriage, the fairy-tale type that usually only came true in between the pages of a romance book.

Seeing a loving relationship your whole life definitely filled a kid's mind up with dreams of princes riding in on their white horses to save the day and whisk his princess into the sunset. Vice versa for me but still the same sentiment.

As I'd grown older though, I decided I liked Captain Kirk's ways of enjoying all the women better than settling down.

But seeing people fall in love left and right around me and having my sisters popping out kids had made me once more crave what I'd wanted as a child.

My very own happily ever after.

When Tara had broken up with me, Mom had hugged me and promised I would find a woman who would appreciate me. Someone unselfish who would fit into my life like the puzzle piece I'd dreamed about once upon a time.

But I'd resorted back to my playboy ways times ten because fuck that shit. I'd also never been more miserable.

Blake rolled up the plans and grabbed a couple of papers off his desk. "Let's go take our morning walk around the job."

As his foreman who'd grown lazy as fuck on the bigger jobsite, I trailed along after him, wishing shit would shift around for the better.

Something needed to stir the pot of my stagnant existence.

Or maybe I needed to make the change.

But what that entailed, I had no clue since I wasn't about to be vulnerable again. Misplacing my loyalty to a woman who would only suck me dry—and not in the good way—then throw me out like yesterday's trash?

That was the last thing I wanted in life.

Chapter 4

Jessica

Cassie ran a raging fever over the weekend and ended up so exhausted that I had to take two more days off work without pay. I'd planned on doing my budget and bills the following Saturday, but when Christine handed me my check right before my lunch break on Friday, I peeked to find it wasn't anywhere near enough to cover my expenses. My shoulders slouched along with my already low mood. Playing catch-up always sucked, and unless I could sign some new customers in the next couple of weeks, I would be in even deeper financial trouble.

Cassie and I would be eating box mac and cheese for the foreseeable future. Maybe I would break up our routine with some fancy ramen noodles topped with chopped, wilted veggies off the discount shelf.

I stuffed my check into my purse and headed to the tiny lunchroom down the business's back hall, worry eating at my insides same as always.

I wanted Cassie to have a better life than me, to enjoy the opportunities my mother hadn't been able to provide. It was bad enough my daughter didn't have a father—and I wasn't interested in finding a fill-in one for her either.

Sitting down at the table, peanut butter and jelly on cheap bread in hand, I blew out a breath between my lips. Men and dating were an absolute joke.

I tore a bite off my sandwich and stared at the water cooler. In a moment of vulnerability and loneliness, I'd tried a dating app but had given up after a week. It seemed every guy on there had only been looking for a hookup—certainly not a ready-made family. Then I'd gotten my head back on straight and reminded myself I couldn't trust another man in our lives. I'd deleted the app and hadn't considered another one since.

I hadn't broken the cycle, but Cassie would. Even if I had to eat unfulfilling carbs until she turned of age to start making her own way in life.

"Hey."

I turned and tried to muster a smile for Christine who'd come into the break room for lunch. "Hey."

Her gaze landed on my sandwich, and she grimaced, her painted lips curling upward.

I shrugged. "It's my fav," I lied, but PB&J was my favorite meal of all the inexpensive food I could afford to fill my kitchen cabinets with.

"Nasty stuff right there." Christine grabbed a container out of the fridge and sat beside me. She popped the lid.

I leaned over for a closer look at her lunch and wrinkled my nose. "Bunny food—sans dressing as usual. Talk about nasty."

Her eyes twinkled. "It's *my* fav."

"Liar," I muttered and bit into my sandwich, surprised to find myself smiling for what was probably the first time that week.

Thank God I'd inherited my mother's fast metabolism and I didn't have to battle the ten pounds that Christine always complained about that lingered on her hips since college. There was no way in hell I could survive on the greens she chose to eat.

"Another letter came in the mail this morning."

Coldness seeped over me at Christine's quiet statement. The hairs on my neck stirred. "Devon?" I asked around my mouthful of sandwich, my voice equally hushed—but from fear rather than needing privacy.

She nodded without looking at me and speared some of her salad. "I opened it and read enough to know it came from him before filing it away with the others. You didn't want to see it, did you?"

I shook my head and tried to swallow what had turned to revolting sludge in my mouth.

Devon had somehow learned where I worked and sent a letter to my attention once a month like clockwork. Christine had happened to catch me opening the first. She'd refused to let me rest until she learned what had drained my face of blood and had me running for the employee bathroom to empty my stomach. Since then, she'd insisted on reading them first and tucking them away...just in case.

Occasionally, a call transferred to me, the dead silence on the other end letting me know it was him.

But there was nothing my only friend could do about his stalking me from jail in that way.

"No, I don't," I managed to whisper after a quick sip of cool water. "Same threats?"

"To hurt you as you hurt him," Christine repeated what he'd written many times before. "It's a good thing he's behind bars."

I nodded, unable to make a response out of the fear for my daughter clogging my throat.

"I'm hanging onto it just like all the others."

I made a noise of agreement while staring at the rest of my sandwich I suddenly had no wish to finish.

Christine heaved a heavy sigh as if to clear the air and shoved a forkful of salad into her mouth. "So. Any plans tonight?" she asked around a mouth of dressing-free greens.

I swigged my water for much-needed moisture and cleared my throat, happy to move on in conversation even though my brain stayed tied up with ropes of fear. "Cartoons and homemade popcorn."

"No hot date?"

I cast a sideways glance at her while snorting, feigning my amusement over her suggestion. "Yeah. Right."

She peered at me for a few long seconds while I forced down the final two bites of my sandwich since I needed the calories and energy to get me through the rest of the day.

"What?" I finally asked Christine while shoving my empty sandwich baggie into my purse for a rinse out at home and fourth or fifth use.

"You need to get laid."

I huffed a sarcastic laugh. "Yeah. I'm starting to forget what a penis looks like."

A slow smile spread over Christine's lips, and the glint in her eyes promised trouble.

"What did you do?" I asked, awareness tingling over me.

"You'll get a front and center reminder tomorrow night." Her grin widened.

"Of what...a penis?" I scoffed and stood, ready to get back to work. "I don't have a date. I'm not even on any app, so it's not happening."

"I bought you an evening with one of the Elite Escorts."

My gaze jerked to her face, and I stalled out from pushing in my chair. Still smiling but with emerald eyes serious as hell, she peered up at me.

"The what?" I asked.

"A male escort. A sex slave whose job is to satisfy your every whim and take care of that tickling itch you've had going on since Cassie came along."

Heat flooded my face—and my body. "Absolutely not. No. Way." The words tumbled from my lips as I shook my head.

"Yes way. Your date and the limo will pick you up tomorrow night at seven."

My spine stiffened. "No."

Christine stuffed more bunny food in her mouth but didn't take her focus off me. "*Yes*," she said around the greens, unladylike same as always.

"I don't have a sitter," I sputtered, clueless as to why I offered an excuse rather than another resounding *no*.

She smiled brightly while chewing and swallowing. "Yes, you do. I'm bringing an overnight bag to your place and crashing on the couch since you won't be home until morning."

"No," I said again, my tone far from firm. "I'm not going out with some...some...man whore."

She laughed and stabbed at her dry salad again. "It's not a date, Jessie. It's simply a chance to get laid. No strings attached."

"I could have done that with any of those guys from that dating site you talked me into."

"Maybe." Her eyes narrowed although the smirk remained on her lips. "But you deserve so much more. A night on the town being wined and dined by a man who's sure to know his way around a woman's body. I even picked out the perfect fantasy man. He's hot with a capital H."

My pulse went from slow to rapid in a blink. We had shared our love of tall, dark, and handsome with Greek god bodies plenty of times over lunch breaks. While hers tended toward being athletes, I could care less about any of the sports she enjoyed. "You didn't."

"Oh, I did." The damn glint appeared in her eyes again. "A pretty one with muscles cut enough to slice through any woman's inhibitions."

A shudder rippled through me, and I shook my head. "You can take my place."

"Nope. I have plans."

"Christine..."

"I already paid. Your cute ass is going. End of." Another pile of spinach and lettuce went into her mouth with finality.

There was no point in arguing with Christine Gemberling when she got her stubborn head stuck on something.

If only I had the nerve to tell my friend I would rather have the cash she'd blown on my date instead. The bills piling on my desk at home needed to be paid a hell of a lot more than I needed masculine hands on my skin and a dick inside my lonely body.

But...

I couldn't deny both of those sounded downright divine.

One night. Just for stress release and some selfish me time.

What was the worst that could happen?

Chapter 5

Reid

He was late. Again.

I pulled into the jobsite's gravel lot and, shaking my head, parked beside the lumber that had been delivered the day before. I cut the engine and sipped my coffee from Dunks, my gaze on the road and watching for Blake and his silver F-250.

I'd been working for my best friend's company, Harper's Construction, since we had graduated from high school. Blake had gotten his bachelor's in business while I'd toiled away for his father, sweating in the summer and freezing my balls off in the winter. I loved construction though. Lifting walls up, rafters, and the smell of sawdust. There was nothing like building something with my own two hands and seeing progress from my hard work every day.

As the years had passed, I went from grunt laborer to foreman once Blake took over the company from his father who had retired a few years earlier. But I still enjoyed getting into the thick of things when I wanted to sweat alongside the other employees while shooting the shit.

My cell dinged from an incoming text from Elite's office, and I put my coffee in the cupholder.

Elite: **New client booked for tonight.**

Client? Brow furrowing over the singular, I punched in my password to access the private file Micah's secretary Dina had attached. Another text came through before I got to read the information.

Elite: **This is not your usual, but Jarod had to cancel, and you're the only other one available who fits the request for tall, dark, and handsome. Please respond ASAP.**

Sometimes specific desires accompanied reservations with Elite, and while Jarod and I could have passed for brothers with our dark hair and eyes, he always got the single ladies. We'd teamed up a couple of times when a woman wanted to fulfill her threesome fantasy—and paid good money to ensure we left her satisfied and smiling.

I flicked back to the file.

A professional photo came up of a half-smiling blonde with light-brown eyes. Zooming in closer brought those gorgeous orbs into sharper focus, and my breath blasted from my lungs like I'd taken a punch to the gut.

The curve of her smile didn't reach her captivating eyes. They were shuttered. Closed off and full of pain.

A desire to shelter and protect swept over me, the kind of instinctive feelings I'd only experienced with my sisters and their kids.

But with ten times the force and...*more.*

I studied the soft curve of her cheekbone, the light arch of her eyebrows, and the tilted-up nose leading down to sensual lips.

"Fuck," I mumbled, shifting at the immediate rush of blood to my groin.

The woman was drop-dead gorgeous without heavy makeup and a painted mouth. Nothing but a lick of mascara enhanced her honey-shaded eyes, and she didn't even need the glisten of gloss to plump up her already perfectly shaped lips.

Hissing, I adjusted my swollen dick.

Hot and hurting, she was my favorite type of kryptonite. Someone who had needs I naturally wanted to give comfort and love to.

"Goddamnit." I tore my focus off the image, zoomed out, and skimmed through the rest of the file Micah's secretary had sent me.

The client's name was listed as Jessica Lindy, but the payee was a name I recognized from years earlier.

I couldn't contain a huffed laugh.

Christine Gemberling, valedictorian of our high school class, the girl who'd slept her way through the football and hockey teams but couldn't be bothered with us baseball players. She'd been one hot girl, full of herself, and confident as fuck.

But she was a redhead, and I'd always preferred blondes.

She'd paid for an overnight for her friend who she said never got to go out. Jessica, Christine claimed in the notes section, deserved to be pampered and loved on, along with being given a handful of climaxes to last her until she decided it was time to live again.

While I didn't usually do one-on-ones for Elite, I swiped back up to the picture of the woman Christine had hired Elite to satisfy. Jessica...her name rolled around in my brain as I searched her face for a hint of recognition.

Nothing pinged a memory, no surety that I'd ever seen her before.

Someone banged on my truck window.

I jerked my head up as adrenaline jolted through my system. My scowl dissolved at the sight of my best friend.

"'Sup, Harper?" I asked while putting the window down.

"Where's mine?" my boss asked with a grin, pointing with his chin toward the large Dunks in my cup holder.

"You make me come into work on a Saturday and expect me to repay you by buying?" I asked and shook my head. "The hell's wrong with you?"

His slow smirk said a story was on its way. "I didn't have time to stop."

"I don't want to know why—"

"Wren jumped into the shower with me, and once she dropped to her knees, I lost track of time."

"Sure you did." I pocketed my cell, grabbed my coffee, and pushed open the truck door wide enough that Blake had to step back and give me three feet.

"You didn't get laid last night?" he asked, shoving his hands in his pockets, a lady-killing smile showing off his perfect teeth I'd always envied.

Two of mine lay a bit higher and longer with pointed tips that sometimes got referred to as fangs. While I didn't care for the look of them, women with vampire fantasies enjoyed the shit out of my biting on their pristine bodies.

"'Course I did," I replied. "Perks of being Micah's employee."

Blake turned toward the foundation we'd poured the week before, and I followed a step behind, my mind going back to the hurt blonde Christine had paid money to show a good time.

A twinge of arousal and excitement slid back through my blood. "Gunna get some tonight too."

He grinned over his shoulder. "Third wheel job treating you well, huh?"

"Enough I won't need this job for much longer. Swinging a fucking hammer all day is starting to wear my ass out," I lied since I only picked one up a couple of days a week as the foreman.

"If pussy takes my top employee from me, I'll kick your ass from here to Foxborough."

"Ha." I sipped my coffee and grinned. "I'd like to see you try."

Blake pulled up short and turned, focusing on my face. He might have had a little bit of height on me, but I outweighed his ass by a good twenty pounds of pure muscle. "You seriously thinking about leaving me?"

"Fuck no." I punched his bicep.

Relief flooded his eyes. "Fucker."

I grinned and lifted my cup. "That's what they pay me for."

Shaking his head, Blake started off again.

"Don't tell me you're missing your freedom," I said, thinking of the woman who'd snagged his heart and balls the summer before.

"Shit, no. Wren is all the woman I'll ever need for the rest of my life."

A shot of jealousy twisted through my stomach same as it usually did when Blake mentioned his girlfriend. We'd shared more than a handful of women in his free days, but the times had changed. Our oat-sowing fun together had long passed.

While I pondered futile daydreams that I would one day find a woman I could give my undivided attention to, I sure as shit wouldn't ever let another man touch her either, same as Blake with his Wren.

No more threesomes.

And even though deep down I wanted the happily ever after with picket fences and all that shit he and my sisters had found, I still wasn't about to hand over my heart to another woman for her to stick a fork into.

Having been sliced and diced with a jagged knife once before, I knew I had to guard myself. That meant no emotions could get tangled up while I went on my first one-on-one for Elite.

No matter how alluring Jessica's hurting golden eyes tempted me to drown in her sorrow and help her find her way back to the surface of living again, I would protect myself.

***

My old classmate had gone all out in her desire to see her friend Jessica spoiled rotten. Elite gave me the limo for the night, a suite at the Kimball's favorite hotel downtown, and the go-ahead to enjoy their five-star French restaurant and a good bottle or two of their best wine.

My ride pulled up in front of an apartment complex forty-five minutes north of Boston, and a quick glance showed me the place was clean—decent. The sun had begun to set, but daffodils and tulips lined the front walkway to the glass double doors, and flowering Nanking cherry bushes hid a couple of AC units with their pink and white blossoms.

I keyed in the apartment number I'd been supplied with on the intercom and waited. Rarely did butterflies take flight in my stomach, but for the first time in a long while, I would be on a date with a single woman—not a date—but still. I took comfort in being the third wheel but with Jessica? I wouldn't have a buffer to hide behind if her emotions got too caught up in the heat of passion.

At the thought of seeing those honey eyes of hers darken with arousal, those plump lips parting on gasps or leaking whimpers, I groaned. Dozens of ways to satisfy Christine's requests, to leave her friend sated and smiling had filled my mind most of the day.

But one rule I decided to etch into my brain for the night blared like a blinking red light.

No kissing.

Reminding myself of that hard limit, I lifted my shaking hand to buzz the intercom again.

All sense of being a professional had fled the building from the moment I'd looked into an image's eyes. What the fuck was I in for when Jessica stood before me?

Cursing, I inhaled fully and slowly exhaled to the count of ten.

"Yes?" a low, breathy voice said as I went to push the intercom button for the third time.

A shot of lust hit my balls low and hard from a mere rasped answer.

"Reid from Elite Escorts here for Ms. Lindy," I said, surprised to hear a slight tremor in my words. *Get a grip.*

"I-I'll be right down." The replying, shaky tone let me know I wasn't the only one nervous about the evening.

A discrete adjustment of my semi and I stepped back, creating plenty of room on the wide stoop for a second person. Unless a woman's body language and eyes begged from the onset, I stayed well out of their personal space. There was nothing worse than someone getting up in your wheels when you wanted three feet.

Unless you were getting paid to let them in.

Clearing my throat, I smoothed down my suit coat, fingering the top button and making sure it was done up properly.

God, what the hell was I thinking when I'd agreed to a one-on-one?

A flicker of movement through the glass door drew my gaze. Golden blonde hair swept over bare shoulders. Smooth, pale skin...

My mouth watered as my gaze dipped lower to lush cleavage and curvy hips hugged by a tiny black dress. Bare legs and high heels...screw the personal space.

I stepped forward to open the door, my head lifting to drink in the rest of Jessica Lindy. Her pale whiskey-brown eyes were even more potent in person, but the wariness and exhaustion pouring from them like wet cement from a flute kept me from moving.

My chest ached for her—a woman I didn't know beyond her name.

"Jessica?" I asked. Our eyes locked on each other, and awareness skittered through every cell in my body.

"Jessie, please." She attempted to tug on a sweater while fumbling with her purse and keeping her focus latched onto my face.

"Allow me," I said, somehow finding the ability to step closer to help her. The warmth of her skin radiated out to kiss my fingers as I held her sweater in place, tempting me to lift her hair out of the way. Instead, I shifted back while she tugged the sweater tight and clutched her purse in front of her.

"Reid Sullivan." I offered my hand, still lost in the swarm of emotion in her expressive eyes.

Jessie hesitated but eventually released her hold on the

purse and slid her cool hand into mine. I went from semi to steel with one breath at the feel of her smooth skin against my callused palms. I lifted our clasped hands and kissed her knuckles.

A small smile curved her lips, easing the pain in her steady gaze. "You're a charmer."

"I aim to please," I told her with a wink.

Light laughter eased the tension between us.

Christine's friend might be hurt, but she was far from insecure and timid. That ensured easier conversation and a means for me to keep my protective instincts locked up where they wouldn't interfere and tempt me to get involved beyond the physical.

Perhaps our "date" wouldn't be so bad after all.

"Shall we?" I asked, tucking her hand into the crook of my arm.

I would give Elite's client the ride of her life, then do what I always did once my paid-for time ended.

Walk away and never look back.

A shiver of something unnameable slid down my spine, but I ignored the sixth sense and led her toward our waiting limo.

Chapter 6

Jessica

S*hall we?*

I held in my snort over Reid's words echoing in my mind.

You've already been bought for the night, I thought about reminding my escort. My nasty attitude had bubbled out at Christine more than once after she'd shown up earlier to babysit—those plans she'd explained that kept her from taking my place. While my pissiness over her meddling remained, I reminded myself not to be unkind to the man beside me who wasn't aware of my circumstances.

As far as I knew, he probably thought I had money to spare, considering he got a paycheck to pick me up and take me out for dinner.

I glanced back at my second-floor apartment window, expecting Christine watched us amble toward the limo. Sure enough, she looked down on us and gave me two thumbs up while mouthing *Have fun!*

I stole a glance up at Reid as I turned forward once more. Tall, dark, and handsome didn't begin to describe the slab of man beef beside me. He towered over my five-foot-five frame. The suit didn't hide his lumberjack shoulders, but it tapered nicely to reveal his trim waist. I'd seen what lay beneath—Christine had made sure to show me the pictures of Reid on Elite's website. Reid, not Jarod, the escort she'd originally picked out for me. Mr. Pretty Boy Jarod had been more to her liking than mine, anyway.

They'd had to switch men due to personal reasons, and Christine hadn't hesitated to agree to the swap. I'd have been perfectly content with giving up the idea altogether, but upon seeing Reid's profile, I'd decided otherwise.

The man was hot. Like, burn your fingertips on an iron hot. Incendiary. Dangerous to the libido and emotional health of an unsuspecting woman who would have all of his attention in the coming hours.

Fresh-shaven, he still sported a dark shadow on his jaw. His hair lay a little longer on top in a slightly wavy, carefree style. His eyes were a rich brown, yet they twinkled like the stars I wished on at night.

Playful, those orbs promised.

Sensual, his low voice whispered, sending teasing caresses over my ears.

Gentle, his touch assured me. Soft, full lips against my knuckles...

My knees had weakened as warmth flooded through me from a mere brush of his mouth over my skin. And the woodsy cologne with a hint of vanilla? My mouth turned into salivation central.

"Nervous?" he asked, squeezing my fingers against the crook of his elbow.

"Honesty is always the best policy," my mom had always declared. Not that I disagreed. Truth on my tongue had caused more than one fight with Devon. "Yes," I replied, putting thoughts of my ex aside.

"Me too."

"Yeah. Okay." I huffed a snort. Nothing about his wide shoulders and the confident tilt of his chin suggested the man had butterflies like I did.

"Honest to God," he murmured, brushing against my side and sending goosebumps skittering all over my body.

He was nothing more than a paid escort, full of shit, saying whatever he felt I needed to hear in order to fulfill his job for the evening.

I ignored Reid's declaration and smiled at the driver as he opened the limo's back door for me.

"Ma'am." He nodded in greeting.

"Thank you." I climbed into the limo as best I could without baring my ass and thong to the world beneath the too-short, tight-as-hell dress Christine had gifted me. Early birthday presents, she'd said. Again, I'd rather have had the cash she'd dished out for it, but I didn't want to sound ungrateful.

I'd ended up tugging off the old skirt and outdated top I'd selected for the night—the clothing she'd frowned at—and poured myself into the piece of restrictive material she called a designer dress.

But I'd felt like a million bucks after seeing myself in the full-length attached to the back of my bedroom door.

Christine had added more eyeliner and shadow to my face than I felt comfortable with, but she'd smudged here and there, dabbed on some blush, and laid on the red lipstick, telling me to shut up and deal.

I figured going all out wasn't any worse than already having agreed to a date with a paid escort, and Christine had assured me I looked smokin'. The compliment earned an eye roll from me.

"So." Reid settled beside me on the back seat, his presence, heavenly scent, and aura of confidence filling the too-small space. Rather than feeling intimidated or uncomfortable though, my body actually melted into the leather beneath my body, my breath emptying my lungs with a deep sigh.

Zero responsibilities lay in wait for me tonight. No bossy-boo to talk into eating dinner. No whining toddler who didn't want to bathe or go to bed.

Christine would have her hands full, but she'd brought it on herself.

The least I could do was enjoy my carefree evening exactly as she'd demanded of me.

"I think a night out is just what the doc ordered," Reid said, his velvet-like voice causing the hairs on my nape to stand on end. Dark and merry eyes studied my face, bringing warmth to my core.

I raised a brow, trying to stifle my ridiculous attraction to the fine specimen of man too close to my side. "I want you to know, my friend put me up to this. Never in a million years would I blow money on a—" I clenched my jaw shut as heat flooded my face. Damn runaway mouth.

"Go ahead." He smirked, the twitch of his lips making me hungry for a taste. "Say it."

"Fine." I met his gaze, unwavering. "Man whore."

"Ouch." He slapped a hand to his chest and rubbed as though my label had stung.

What a way to begin the evening. Me and my big mouth, spewing out words without thinking them through first.

Might as well lay it all out there and set the ground rules before anything got started.

My chin lifted. "I have no intention of sleeping with you."

"Fine by me." The corner of his mouth twitched again, and my PMS-ing emotional inner bitch wanted to read into his meaning.

Wasn't I pretty enough for him to get it up? Did I look like a lousy lay? Devon had said it often enough I heard his words echoing in my ears.

"Glad we got that cleared up," I snapped, jerking my attention to the window and the setting sun.

Silence settled over us but without discomfort. Devon's angry words continued to play through my mind, and I found my eyes filling with tears. I was dressed to kill—or so I'd thought—with a sure lay if I'd been up for using the guy's dick to get off. A completely paid-for date, and all I could think about was my ex.

"Who was he?" Reid's soft voice pulled me from the troubled thoughts I struggled to force away.

"Who was who?" I asked, turning to peer up at his face that no longer held a trace of twinkling amusement.

"The one who put the haunted hurt in your eyes."

"Ouch," I copied his word, lifting a hand to my chest.

Reid's gaze didn't waver. "Beautiful doe-like, whiskey-colored eyes. Far from unattractive." He ran the back of his finger down my cheek, making my nipples tighten. "Intriguing, actually."

I found myself wanting to lean into his touch as though the soft caress of his hand could soothe away every hurt Devon had inflicted on my mind and emotions. But there was no such thing as a magic touch or healing balm in fingertips. Or lips. Especially not dicks.

"Tell me," Reid said again, lacing his fingers through mine with a calm assurance of safety I'd never felt before and certainly couldn't fathom.

"I thought you were supposed to show me a good time

tonight." I tried and failed to keep the bitterness from my tone. The poor man didn't deserve to reap what Devon had sown.

"I'm a great listener." His sweet smile melted a little of the ice that encased my heart. "Hell"—he all-out grinned—"I'm a handy man to have in your back pocket if the need for revenge ever comes knockin'. I'll give you my card just in case."

I laughed. No clue why, but the sincerity of his offer baffled yet delighted me. "You really want to know the shit of my life?" I asked, angling on the seat to face him better.

His smile faded as he continued to study my eyes as though seeking out the deepest secrets I held inside my head and heart. "You need to unload what's troubling you, Jessie, or I'll never get you to enjoy this evening like you should. Rant. Rail on me. Take out the aggression leashed inside of your heart."

My gaze narrowed. "Did Christine put you up to this?"

"Your friend paid for my time this evening, but that's it. *This* is me." He tapped what had to be hard-as-rock pecs beneath the suit coat. "Reid Sullivan asking a beautiful young woman to unburden her mind. Share her hurt and let someone try to erase it for a few hours. And if that's all we get to tonight"—he leaned toward me, those dark eyes of his radiating honesty and assurance—"then I'll be happy to offer more of my own time to sate your body as well."

Warmth flooded through me, easing some of the cold bitterness I'd lived with for far too long. "It's a long story," I said.

"I'm all ears."

"I'll probably cry and make a mess of the face Christine painted on me."

"I'll bet you're even more beautiful without all the makeup."

My face flushed at our quick back and forth. "Stop already."

His white teeth flashed brightly in the car's dim interior, tingling the lonely space between my thighs. The man had a killer smile with canines just prominent enough to be alluring. Enough to make even the most cold-hearted bitch cave to his whims.

I started at the beginning.

Chapter 7

Reid

She didn't shed a damn tear for the next thirty or so minutes on our way into Boston. Inner strength shone through her like a living force of energy, lighting her up from the inside out. I'd never been so damn poetic about a woman in my life, but there was no other way to describe the hot package wrapped up in a clingy black dress beside me.

Her eyes flashed, brows furrowed, and lips pursed during her painful tale of a poor childhood without a father —similar to Blake's woman. Jessie had learned how to be independent, and her determination to be more than her mom was truly inspiring.

But she'd gotten tangled up with an abusive asshole, the type who knew how to manipulate and make her stay. Fury made her bristle while telling me about Devon, the way he'd treated her, and the disappointment she felt in herself for allowing the man to have so much presence in her life even after he got locked up and she'd been granted the divorce two years later.

I kept my thoughts to myself concerning the whole affair, not wanting to upset her further.

When Jessie turned her story to the love of her life, Cupid's bow found me hard and fast. Like a hammer to the thumb, a two-by-four to the head...goddamn, did I reel from the blow. Anger over her asshole ex faded away as she told me about her daughter.

"Her name is Cassie." Jessie's face softened, the love in her eyes I'd seen countless times in all my sisters'. "I call her mini-me since she looks just like I did at that age."

"How old is she?" I asked, curling my hands into fists to keep from touching Jessie's skin which appeared fragile and translucent and in need of tender loving care.

"She just turned three in March. She's a little spitfire like me too." She laughed, her whiskey-brown eyes sparkling with life for the first time since I'd met her on the stoop of her apartment building. "Her favorite words are 'No way!' which flies out of her mouth at least a dozen times a day."

I couldn't keep from smiling. "Outspoken already, huh?"

"Mini-me." Jessie laughed again and shrugged.

Staring into her face, I decided hearing that sound every day for the rest of my life wouldn't be a hardship. A rush of adrenaline and excitement once more swept through my blood. I shoved against the draw that felt more potent than a sweating bottle of beer after a long day's work laboring beneath the sun.

I'd helped Tara smile again, only to have her return the gift of love and acceptance by breaking my heart.

Keep the emotions in check, I reminded myself, unable to stop from drinking in the happiness on Jessie's face that made me want to dream about a fulfilling ending to my life's story no matter how badly I needed to tend to my own heart first.

"She's my reason for living—the *only* one. After Devon..." Another flash of hurt filled Jessie's eyes, stirring up my anger and making me want to wrap her up in my arms.

"Asshole." I hadn't meant to voice my opinion but it slipped out.

Light laughter brought the sparkle back to her eyes. "That's milder of a name than he deserves. I shouldn't allow the wounds he's caused inside of me to control my future, but it's impossible for me to trust anyone."

I couldn't help myself or stop the need to touch her running desperately through my blood. I tucked a strand of blonde hair behind her ear, my fingertips grazing her lobe. She stilled, her lips parting slightly. The idea she felt the sexual energy between us as deeply as I did roused all sorts of sensual shit up inside my head.

Drugging kisses.

Heavy caresses over shivering skin.

Tasting every inch of her...the gentle slope of her neck, the swell of her breasts, the sweetness between her thighs.

But I'd promised to listen first.

"Deep emotional pain is hard to get past," I murmured, ignoring my swelling dick. "Even when you think you're good to go, a simple circumstance can pick at the not-so-healed scab."

She peered at me. "You've been hurt?"

All thoughts of getting my hands on Jessie fled.

Shrugging, I considered my words and the knife-like action in my gut over memories I'd tried to move past but hadn't ever succeeded. "Not nearly as bad as you but enough that I too find trusting the opposite sex with my heart an impossibility."

"I'm sorry."

God*damn*, did I want to drown in her expressive eyes. Sink into the warmth of her body. Taste the passion sizzling between us on the surface of her lips.

The limo slowed, and I cleared my throat. "Hungry?"

"Yes." Her smile reappeared, dazzling and addictive in its effect on me. "Actually, I am."

I laced my fingers through hers and squeezed, loving how our hands fit together, how she allowed my claiming hold even though I had no such thing on her. "Then let's go take advantage of Elite's tab and toast to your night out."

JE

"Can I ask you a personal question?"

My brow rose. Unlike my usual clients, Jessie seemed to want to chat the night away like I'd encouraged—but not just about her. She'd already learned the names of my three sisters and my five nieces and nephews. "Pretty sure I've told you all there is to know about me," I said and swallowed down the last of the second bottle of red wine we'd enjoyed over our three-hour dinner in the hushed restaurant.

She propped her elbow on the small, round table between us and rested her chin in her palm. "Why did you become an escort?"

I chuckled, and she laughed with me, both of us definitely buzzed enough to relax and speak the truth rather than hide ourselves away. "Because I'm an excellent third wheel."

"Third wheel?"

"Threesomes."

"Oh." Her eyes widened a heartbeat later, and she sat back. "*Oh*," she repeated with obvious clarity of my explanation hitting her brain.

"It was my best friend's idea, really," I offered the reason behind my choice. Well, one of them, anyway.

"Your day job boss, right?" she asked for clarity of what I'd already shared with her.

"Blake. Yeah." I wiped my mouth with my linen napkin and set it to the side of my plate.

"So." She nibbled on her lower lip for a second. "Have you...you know...joined him and his girlfriend?"

"Only once, but that was before they were together for the long haul." I studied Jessie's face as her smile faded, and she glanced away toward the empty tables around us.

"You're a professional third wheel." She spoke the truth of what I did during the night hours, a twinge of unease in my stomach over her quiet tone.

"Yes."

"But you also do one-on-one dates for Elite too?"

"No."

Jessie turned to face me, a line appearing between her arched eyebrows. "No?"

"You're my first."

She sucked in a side of her cheek as though chewing on the soft flesh inside. "Do you have any choice in the matter when Elite schedules a client with you?"

"I do."

Silence hovered again as she stared at me, soft instrumental music sounding from somewhere overhead. I fought not to shift in my chair as I waited for her to get to her point.

"So why me?" she finally asked.

"Why you, what?"

"Why did you agree to this?" she asked, motioning between us with a hand.

I leaned forward, holding her gaze. "Because of the haunted eyes in your profile picture. It was like your soul reached through the image and begged my protective instincts to take you in my arms. I wanted to see happiness on your face. Satisfaction and satiated bliss, which after learning more about you, I believe you definitely deserve."

Her lips parted as she sucked in a breath, her pupils dilating.

I had decided to keep sex off my agenda for the night—unless she suggested or hinted at the desire for more than a friendly dinner. Up to that point, I'd done a damn good job of keeping my thoughts about what I wanted to do to her and those sweet curves of hers to myself.

I'd been the ear I'd promised, rejecting all the sexual advances my mouth longed to spew. Ignoring the continuous throb in my balls had proven just as difficult.

The obvious arousal in her eyes made continuing with both of those choices almost near impossible. I allowed my gaze to slide down over her chest, watching hard nubs appear beneath the clingy fabric.

Swallowing hard, I forced my focus back up, a brow raised in question.

Pink flushed Jessie's cheeks as she reached for her wine glass that held nothing more than a single swallow. "I'm not going to sleep with you."

I couldn't help my grin over her breathless declaration. "You want to though."

She shrugged and sipped.

Needing to let the issue go and stick to my guns, I settled on the next best option. "You have me until morning,

Jessie. Is there anything—besides sex—I can do to help you forget about reality for just a little while?"

"A body rub and foot massage." The words blurted from her lips, and the flush on her cheeks deepened.

"Your wish is my command." I stood, tossed my napkin onto the table, and held out my hand before she could take her request back.

She peered up at me, seeming stunned by my fast move to give her what she'd asked for. "Where are we going?"

"Trust me." I wiggled my fingertips at her in encouragement to put her pleasure in my hands.

She hesitated a few more seconds before gathering her purse and accepting my offer.

I didn't have the option to lose myself in her sweetness or feel her climax around my aching dick, but I sure as hell was going to touch every inch of her skin she would allow.

Chapter 8

Jessica

"Where are we going?" I asked for a second time as Reid led me through the crazy-expensive restaurant and back toward the hotel's lounge.

"Upstairs."

My heart thudded in my chest, and I was all too aware of the dampness coating my panties. "Upstairs. As in a room."

"Yes."

"You don't need to go through any trouble—"

"Elite has supplied the accommodations, and we have it until morning," he said, his hand tightening around mine. "A limo will pick us up out front at eight tomorrow."

Christine had said I wouldn't be back that night, but I hadn't expected to really spend the entire evening in a hotel room. "No sex," I whispered as we approached the main desk.

"I promise I'll keep my dick to myself," he whispered back.

I chewed on the inside of my cheek again as Reid spoke

with a young woman behind the desk, signed something, and accepted a card key.

On unsteady legs, I followed him into the elevator. The doors swished shut behind us, and I swallowed against my sudden nerves. *No sex, no sex,* I chanted with each heartbeat. *I'm not getting caught up in this too-hot, too-sweet escort.*

The words twisted my stomach, and I grimaced. He didn't seem like a whore—not that I had any clue how a prostitute ought to behave. I'd expected a suave, full-of-bullshit womanizer who would earn his pay, but Reid seemed open and candid. He hadn't held back with any answer to the hundred questions I'd thrown at him.

But why get to know a paid escort, I wondered to myself not for the first time since we had sat down to dinner and got submerged in easy conversation. It wasn't like I would be seeing him after our one night together. I couldn't afford even an hour of his time on my measly paycheck. It had just seemed rude to keep the topics on me, and he was so easy to talk to.

He seemed like a sweetie. But, Devon had too in the beginning.

Reid smiled at me, his dark eyes full of more than mere friendliness, his panty-melting smile efficient in earning every dollar Christine had paid for him.

My thong did a lousy job of containing my body's immediate reaction to having his attention radiating down on me. I clenched my thighs together while offering a wobbly smile of my own, images of him crowding me against the elevator door and ravishing my mouth vivid in my mind.

"You don't need to be nervous," he said, his low voice making my nipples pebble again.

"I know that, but my body isn't in agreement with my head." My tone had gone all breathless, but I didn't bother trying to hide my want.

He chuckled and squeezed my fingers. "So you *do* think I'm hot."

I huffed and faced the elevator's opening doors. "A woman would have to be dead to not be turned on by your smile, those twinkly eyes full of mischief, and your carpenter shoulders. Never mind all the muscles that probably lay beneath your perfectly tailored suit."

Releasing another chuckle, he lightly touched my back and led me down a long hallway. He paused before a door, slid in the card key, and pushed on the handle. "After you." His rumbled voice promised all sorts of shenanigans, whatever my little heart desired.

No sex.

My body disagreed with my mind, fully primed and ready to gladly welcome whatever he packed in those slacks deep inside my core.

Swallowing hard, I pushed the thoughts of dick from my mind. I'd never been able to keep my emotions from getting all tangled up when sharing my body with a man. It would be safest for me to enjoy the massage he promised and leave it at that.

I stepped past him into a hotel room I'd only seen the likes of in movies and magazines. Leather couches suggested supple comfort, but it was the huge windows overlooking Boston's downtown that beckoned me forward. I moved across the sunken sitting area, soaking in the dark skyline and glittering lights as Reid turned on the dimmers overhead. "What a view," I murmured, knowing I would never see its likes again.

"A hell of one." His suggestive tone had me glancing

over my shoulder. His gaze roamed my backside, and the want in his eyes made my knees wobble. He stalked forward like a lion, ensnaring me with his dark eyes.

I held my breath, unsure of his intent, every inch of me desiring the same thing smoldering in his gaze.

He stopped short of touching me, and the energy crackled between us, stealing my breath. I stared up at him, my pulse thrumming. Trembling beneath the onslaught of his woodsy cologne and sheer presence, I waited. Unsure. Unsteady. And unable to stop my craving for his touch showing in my expression.

"Ready for that massage?" he asked quietly, the brush of knuckles down my cheek rushing moisture to coat my panties and cloud my ability to process a single thought.

"W-what?"

"Massage and foot rub. That's what you want, isn't it?"

I bit my inner lip over his sinfully slow smirk. It took my brain a few seconds to come back online and remember why we'd come up to the room. I managed a dumb nod.

Flashing a grin, he brushed his thumb across my parted lips.

A moan escaped me as my eyelids fluttered shut.

"I don't usually kiss clients, but I want my lips on you, Jessie," he murmured. "Say the word, and I'll give you whatever you want."

Nope. No way. Not even a little caress of his mouth.

"One kiss," I heard myself whisper, knowing I damned myself to hell and heartache.

Soft, warm lips brushed against mine without hesitation, and I sagged against his hard body. *Oh. My. God.* His sweet breath, the slow and gentle pressure of his full lips... everything inside me melted into liquid warmth.

It had been so long since I'd been good and truly kissed,

but no one had ever emptied my mind and filled me up with pure, unadulterated need. Arousal swirled through me like I'd never known existed, settling between my thighs and bringing another moan to my vocal cords.

Reid stepped closer, one palm resting on my hip, the heat of his skin burning through the thin dress. He slid his other hand up my neck and tangled it in my hair, gently tugging my head to the side with a slight hint of dominance.

Something I told myself I wouldn't ever allow myself to fall beneath again.

A flick of Reid's tongue against my lower lip, and my body granted his request without thought of self-preservation or concern for my well-being. I opened, and we both groaned as our tongues came together and parted, dancing in time with the thumps of my heart.

Mere lips had been breathtaking. Stroking tongues and gentle nibbles took his kiss to another atmosphere, a place that offered mindless euphoria. I became a puddle of thawed ice, quickly warming to the boiling point.

Reid kept his hands on my lower back and in my hair while I mapped out his back, shoulders, and chest, desperate to feel the heat of his skin on mine. So firm...hard muscle...I couldn't begin to imagine how drool-worthy his body was beneath the fitted suit.

Reid pulled away too damn soon, leaving me panting and needy to the point a mere touch to my clit would cause absolute rapture to shudder through my body. We stared at each other in the dim light, Reid with a hesitant smile, me a trembling, horny mess of a woman who couldn't catch her breath.

Clearing his throat, he stepped back and released his hold on me. "Go into the bedroom and take your clothes off. There are towels in the adjoining bathroom. Wrap one around yourself and get comfy on that big-ass bed, belly down."

I blinked, processing the words that had sounded ragged and wrapped up in hot sex.

Uh...oh yeah. Massage. Right.

Unable to find my voice, I nodded and tried to walk around him. My heels proved dangerous, and I almost went sprawling to the floor.

"Here. Let me." Reid dropped to his knees and unbuckled the black heels Christine had insisted I wear.

I grabbed hold of Reid's shoulder to stop myself from falling over, my gaze locked on the dark head inches away from my throbbing core. Thoughts of him lifting my dress's hem with his teeth brought a moan to my throat, but I bit down on the inside of my lip to keep from letting it out.

And begging him to put his mouth on me.

His large hand slid up my calf and back down before making short work of the clasp. My foot slid free, and he ran his hand up my other leg, catching my breath again.

Get a grip, Jessie.

The barest touch of his fingertips on my skin was hotter than any sex I could remember. My body craved more. One little lick, one little pinch on my clit, and I'd be screaming my release for the entire hotel to hear.

"Go on," Reid murmured, standing with easy grace and stepping back, my heels dangling from his hand.

With another thoughtless, dumb nod, I managed to make my feet move me forward. I eyed the massive bed while making my way across the bedroom to the open bathroom door. Images of Reid's ass clenching with each thrust into my writhing body flashed across my mind.

"G-good God," I whispered and swallowed hard as a spasm of intense need rocked through my core.

Hands shaking, I all but ripped off my tight dress and restricting bra but paused to consider my panties. A full body massage...

Another few seconds of indecision and I slid the soaked bit of silk off my legs.

Because they'd become uncomfortable, I told myself while wrapping a white fluffy towel around me. A peek into the bedroom revealed it empty, so I scooted to the bed, pulled back the comforter and top sheet, and lay face down a little ways from the edge. I clenched my eyes shut, and my pulse pounded with desperation.

Closer than a hair to hyperventilation, I focused on slowing my breathing and relaxing my muscles. Soft instrumental music floated through the bedroom's closed door, making my seemingly impossible task slightly easier.

"Jessie?" Reid's low voice raised what little hair I had on my body. "Can I come in?"

I squeaked a reply but had to clear my throat and try again. "Yes."

Yes. Please come...I mean, come in. Touch me. Make me come.

Chapter 9

Reid

My gaze ran from Jessie's feet up the pale, creamy skin to the towel wrapped around her midsection and hiding the globes of her ass from my starved sight. Her head faced toward me, eyes clenched shut. A shudder rippled down through her as I drew close.

The scent of her arousal slammed into me like a sledgehammer, and I inhaled deeply, filling my lungs as waterworks went to town in my mouth. Swallowing rather than having drool drip down my chin, I attempted to slow my thumping heart and heavy breathing.

"Comfortable?" I asked, noting her thighs pressed tightly together.

"Mmm hmm." Her murmur sounded like a hummed yes to me, but she lay like rigor mortis had set in.

"Just relax," I murmured. "I'll take good care of you."

I'd left the bedroom door open so the music I'd turned on would help set the mood. Elite's staff had already made the room ready for our arrival. Everything from massage oil to lubes and a handful of toys had been packed into the case

I'd rifled through in the living area while Jessie had gone into the bedroom to take her clothes off.

She didn't move a muscle as I rid myself of my suit coat, loosened my tie, and rolled up my shirt sleeves.

Wishing I could strip entirely and press my body weight against her, I snapped open the cap of a bottle and dripped oil from the back of her creamy white thighs to her ankles. A decent squirt onto my palm, and I recapped and tossed the container on the far side of her stretched-out form. "Cold?" I asked, rubbing my hands together and kneeling on one leg on the bed beside her.

"No," she whispered, the throbbing pulse in her neck tempting me to latch my teeth onto her pale skin.

With firm but gentle pressure, I began working her left foot, digging my thumbs into her arch.

"Oh my God, that feels good," Jessie muttered, the furrow between her brows dissipating, her legs finally relaxing and opening the slightest bit.

I grinned and continued my ministrations without a word. I ran my hands up her calf, spreading the droplets of oil kissing her skin. The darkness beneath the towel's edge called to me. Like a bloodhound on the trail of a hot-blooded meal, I salivated, my cock hardened and ready to slide into her silky heat.

With each upward sweep of my hands, I imagined pressing into her pussy. I'd been hard on and off since first picking Jessie up, and the thought of the sexless night ahead had me thinking I'd probably need a little self-massage of my own in the bathroom once I finished with her.

Over the back of her knee, up to the edge of the towel, I smoothed the oil along her muscles with my thumbs. I rubbed back down a little ways and started upward once more, pushing the towel an inch higher with each pass.

I checked to make sure her eyes remained closed before dipping my head down in hopes to catch a glimpse of her hidden heaven.

It was too damn dark beneath that towel.

A shuddering sigh escaped Jessie's parted lips as I slid my hands beneath it and worked her upper thigh. Deep inhales filled my senses with the musky scent of her arousal, and fuck, did I want a taste.

Shifting my knee a little closer to her didn't help create any more room in my slacks for my hard-as-rock cock straining against the fabric, but it made reaching for her opposite thigh more comfortable. I started at the top of her right leg, fingers so damn close to her pussy that her hips lifted the slightest bit with every upward rub of the base of my palms.

"How are you feeling, Jessie?" I asked, my low voice full of lust.

"Amazing," she said, drawing the word out with a groan and spreading her legs slightly wider. "A girl could get used to this."

"You're an incredible woman and deserved to be spoiled. Don't settle for anything less." I moved my hands down to the back of her knee, peeking again beneath the towel I'd managed to rumple. Bare, pink flesh, glistening with welcoming moisture met my needy gaze.

Thank fuck for self-control.

Swallowing hard, I kept my palms moving along her calf, to her ankle, and eventually her foot, my gaze glued the entire time to the wetness seeping from between the swollen lips of her pussy.

"I'm going to pull down the towel to your waist so I can massage your back," I managed to choke out while releasing her foot.

"M'kay."

Every inch of bared flesh called out to my tongue, but I held myself in check, thinking of Jessie—her worries and cares, her need for pampering. Besides, I was a man of my word and had promised no sex. That didn't mean I wouldn't see how far she was willing to go though.

I leaned over her body to reach for the oil, making sure my hard-on blatantly brushed against her thigh. She didn't flinch or shy away, I noted with satisfaction.

Oil pooled where her back gave way to flared hips, and I set to work spreading the slickness up and down the length of her, focusing on the hint of muscles bracketing her spine. Seconds of palming her waist and circling my thumbs along her hip bones turned into minutes as I forced the knots of her lower back to release.

The towel gave way fully, and I moved my hands along with it to massage the perfect globes of her ass. I focused on her face and slid my thumbs down the top of her crack. Her lips parted on a quick inhale, but rather than squeezing her cheeks together like I expected her to, she lifted her hips off the bed as if inviting further exploration.

I made the same sweeping action but pressing wide with my palms, pulling her cheeks apart enough for a peek at her little rosebud. Her moan accompanied the slide of my thumbs along either side of the puckered skin.

"This alright?" I asked, my voice low.

"Yes," she whispered without hesitation.

Jessie ground her hips into the bed and shuddered a third time, her breath coming fast and heavy. Her brow furrowed, cheeks flushed. Moisture dripped from her pussy onto the sheet beneath.

I almost gave in to the temptation to dive down headfirst and lap up her cream. God knew her body's response to my hands said she'd let me eat her out, but like a true gentleman, I kept my fucking promises.

My thumbs brushed the edges of her rosebud, and she gasped, goosebumps pebbling her skin. Oiled and slick, my thumb could press right past her ring of muscle with no resistance if I attempted to breach her body. The temptation of her responsiveness about drove me fucking insane.

Another squeeze of her ass and I slid the pad of my thumb lightly across her hole with a teasing stroke. "Okay?" I checked in again.

"God yes." A deep groan came from her lips, and she shuddered, grinding her hips. I swept back up and over with slightly more pressure.

Her body convulsed. "Oh, God, oh, God." She pressed her face into the mattress, hands grasping at the sheets beside her as she came, the mattress stifling her cries.

Fuck yeah.

I bit my lip and continued to run my thumb across her hole as pre-cum oozed from my throbbing dick.

One last shudder rippled down her body, and I skimmed my hands all the way up her back to her shoulders. Tension began to gather beneath my fingers as her head turned toward the opposite side of the bed.

"I-I'm sorr—"

"Shh. Relax," I said, leaning in to nuzzle her warm ear. "You're beautiful when you let go."

She melted beneath my touch again, and I decided to push a little more. "If you want to roll over, I'll massage your front."

Slow, but without hesitation, Jessie twisted and rolled, her eyelids fluttering open. I nearly lost myself in her sleepy, satisfied whiskey eyes.

I traced my fingers along her collarbone, our gazes

locked, the sound of our breathing drowning the music coming from the other room. Moving my hands lower, I brushed my palms along the tops of her breasts.

Her lips parted.

My gaze trailed along with my hands, over the swollen sides of her full breasts. Her nipples firmed beneath my stare. I circled my thumbs closer, and her areolas pebbled tightly.

I swallowed down against the need to suck the hard nubs soft again and glanced up to find Jessie's eyes had closed. My attention turned to the askew towel covering her pussy and one hip bone and how I could get it to move without actually baring her myself.

I brushed my thumbs along the bottom of her nipples, and she arched into my touch with a quick breath. Smirking and on the verge of combustion, I palmed the undersides of her breasts and kneaded, gently running my fingers across both hard nubs at the same time.

Jessie released a deep groan, her hands grasping at the sheets again.

I rolled the hard peaks between my fingers, waiting as each rise of her hips revealed more of her hip and thigh.

"H-holy shit." She gasped. "I'm going to come again."

Pinching her nipples brought another cry of release that rolled over me like a tsunami. I gritted my teeth to keep from ripping off my slacks and pounding into her.

The towel slipped free from Jessie's core as one last tremor rippled through her, and my gaze zeroed in on the bare swell at the top of her splayed thighs. I slid my slickened hands over her stomach, noting a few stretch marks, but honed in on the cream coating her thighs and swollen lips of her pussy. Her erect clit.

Talk about fucking drool.

The sweet scent of her brought my inner caveman front-and-center, and all I could think was I just might shoot off in my pants without stimulation. Fighting for control, I spanned her waist with my hands and moved them down, my thumbs gliding along her pubic bone and the insides of her thighs.

Eyes clenched shut, Jessie shifted as though restless beneath my touch. Her brow furrowed, lower lip caught between her teeth.

I brushed a knuckle up and over her soaked lips, and she pressed into my touch. An invitation if I'd ever seen one.

"Can I touch you here?"

"Mmmhmm."

"I need words, Jessie."

She swallowed hard. "Yes."

I swept my thumb over her clit, and she gasped, eyelids flying open. Her gaze latched onto me.

I circled her hardened nub with my thumb and dragged the pad down over the top into her slick folds. Her deep groan and the haze of desire in her eyes...

Fuck, did I want her. "Should I stop?" I forced myself to ask.

"No," she whispered, hips rising in invitation.

Her cream coated my exploring fingers, and when she lifted her hips again, I slid one inside of her tight sheath.

So. Fucking. Warm.

My dick ached to burrow in and make itself at home.

Teeth clenched, I pulled out and pressed in with a second finger.

Pupils dilated, mouth open and panting, Jessie stared at me as I fucked into her tight pussy with my fingers. Her breath came in gasps, her inner walls tightening around me so slick and hot I fought to keep a groan contained.

One more, I thought, running my thumb over her clit as I buried my fingers deep inside her again and curled them.

Her pussy clenched down, and her eyes closed, back arching as a third climax rolled over her.

Fuck, Jessie coming was a hell of a thing to behold. Flushed cheeks, parted lips panting for oxygen, and those noises...

"So good," I murmured with a ragged tone, stroking her through her spasms until she lay spent.

Jessie glowed like the sun, blindingly brilliant. A small smile accompanied her sleepy blinking up at me.

I wanted a taste...

Slipping my fingers from her body, I shoved them between my lips before I could be tempted to take her mouth. Her cum hit my tongue with a tangy sweetness unlike anything I'd ever tasted.

Fucking hell. I swallowed hard, my balls throbbing and tight inside their prison, desperate for release.

A full-on sigh shuddered through Jessie, and she went completely lax, her eyelids fluttering shut.

I pulled the top sheet and comforter up over her body before I broke my promise to keep my dick to myself.

She turned her face, cheek pressing against the mattress as though seeking out a gentle caress over her face.

I leaned down and brushed my lips across the hair plastered to her temple. "Sleep," I whispered.

Within seconds, she did as told, soft pants huffing past her parted lips.

Knowing my self-control neared its end—and the fact I'd be unable to keep from hollering the second I jerked off in the bathroom close by—I grabbed my suit coat and left the bedroom, softly closing the door behind me.

My shaft and balls ached to the point of pain, but I

ignored the discomfort and fished my card from my pocket. I stared down at the crisp rectangle of paper in my hand. I couldn't stay the night and not fuck every hole in her body. There was no fucking way.

But, I wanted to see Jessie again.

Goddamned kryptonite.

I scribbled my cell number on the back of the card and left it sitting on top of her purse. Within two minutes, I righted the bag supplied by Elite, took it in hand, and left the hotel room, cursing my inability to be a selfish asshole with every step.

Chapter 10

Jessica

I stretched beneath my blankets, ecstatic that for the first time since her birth, Cassie had slept through the night.

Cracking open an eyelid brought reality into sharp focus, making my smile fade. Sunlight broke over Boston's skyline outside the window I faced, bathing me in warmth.

The previous night came back in a rush as I blinked the buildings into focus, and I sat up, clutching the sheet to my chest. No Reid. The other side of the bed hadn't even been slept in. The alarm clock read seven AM.

We had another hour until the limo would pick us up out front.

I yanked the comforter off the bed and wrapped it around me. No sounds came from the bathroom. Reid wasn't in the living area either, nor was there a trace of another person having spent the night in the suite Elite had paid for.

Disappointment wormed its way into my mind, but I huffed a breath at myself while heading back into the bedroom. "He's an escort. What'd you expect?" I muttered to myself while staring out over Boston's skyline. "Breakfast in bed? Good morning kisses? Cuddles until the last possible second?"

The truth sucked, but I shuffled into the bathroom and turned on the four shower jets to full blast—and hot. I forced my face to relax. Reid Sullivan's absence wasn't worth my frown. I'd had an amazing night full of good conversation, laughter, and the most incredible orgasms I'd ever experienced.

Water sprayed on me from all sides, and I closed my eyes, remembering the feel of his strong hands caressing over me. Sure and steady, he'd brought me release time and again without much effort.

I couldn't even imagine having his entire body involved...

"Oh hell." Whimpering over my mind attempting to do that very thing, I gave myself free rein to enjoy. Feel. Find release while fantasizing about having him between my thighs. His tongue on mine, those calloused fingers mapping out my skin as he thrust into me over and over, heightening my pleasure until I shattered.

Twice.

Pruned like a grape and unsteady on my legs, I climbed out of the shower, dressed in my clothes from the night before, and readied to go home. At ten of eight, I retrieved my heels and purse from the sunken living area where they'd been left before Reid had wrecked my world in the best way possible. A card fluttered to the floor.

Reid Sullivan, Elite Escort in simple black script on a snowy white card, I noted while crouching down to pick it up.

Nice, I thought with sarcastic snark. He'd left his calling card. Unable to help myself, I lifted it to my nose, hoping for a sniff of his cologne. Zero hint of woodsy vanilla deliciousness filled my lungs. Sighing, I flipped the card over and found a phone number along with *My cell* scrawled in blue ink.

I stared for a few seconds, fingertip tapping the card. An invitation to call, obviously, but why? He knew I couldn't afford to book him for another night. More disappointment swept through me as another frown dented my forehead. I stuffed the card in my purse and hurried out to meet the limo.

My evening playing Cinderella had ended.

It was time to get back to the reality of my sad life where Prince Charming and glass slippers didn't exist.

𝕴𝕴

I walked into my apartment and dropped my purse onto the table where Christine sat nursing a steaming mug.

"Hair freshly washed...no makeup and yet glowing." One of her eyebrows rose, and she sipped her coffee while glancing over the rest of me. "If it weren't for that scowl on your face, I'd be tempted to think you enjoyed your night away from responsibility."

Flopping into the chair across from her, I bent to get the heels off my feet. "How was she?"

"Fussed a little last night when it was time for bed, woke briefly at three but then slept until seven. That out of the way, how *was* it?"

"We had an enjoyable ride to the restaurant. Would you believe Reid asked about and seriously wanted to know who had hurt me?"

"I didn't say a word, promise."

I smiled at my friend before getting back up to get

myself a cup of coffee. "I'm not good at hiding my emotions from my face, and Reid just happens to be a decent people reader."

"So did you spill your guts to a complete stranger or did you focus on having a good time?"

I huffed a laugh, got a warm mug in my hands, and sat back down. "I spewed all my past shit and felt a lot better afterward. Then came dinner which was delicious." Sipping, I pretended to be done with my tale.

Christine waited but not for very long. "Details, Jessie. I need to hear all about his dick and if he knew how to use it."

"We didn't have sex." Not really.

She stared, her eyes widening. "Um...*what*?"

"No sex," I repeated and sipped my coffee.

"What did you do all night?" she asked, her tone higher than its usual rasp.

"I allowed him to kiss me, he gave me one hell of a massage, and I came three times."

One of her eyebrows arched. "But no dick was involved?"

"Nope."

"Fingers? Tongue?"

"Yes, fingers and no tongue."

"Sounds like sex to me."

I shrugged.

Slouching in her chair, she propped her elbow on the table, chin in her palm. "Woman, I don't know how you kept your hands off that man. I got an eyeful out the window last night. Reid is fine as hell."

I sipped again, withholding my thoughts on the man.

"Don't give me that shit. He was hot. Great body even in a suit. Those shoulders. Dark hair. Tight ass."

"You speak no lies," I murmured, giving her that at least.

She'd always been quick to edify and drop compliments though.

"Did you have a good time, Jessie?"

"I did. One of the best nights of my life." I realized as I made the claim that I spoke the truth. The draw, the sexual energy, the meal, his hands, his mouth...it would be so easy to get caught up in such a man.

"Then that's all that matters." Christine smiled. "How do you feel this morning?"

"Relaxed, and I can't thank you enough."

"My pleasure."

I considered telling her about the card Reid had left that included a cell number, but since I wasn't sure what to do with that information—and knowing Christine would demand I call him up to see what he had on offer—I held my peace. "Where's Cassie?"

"Your little cutie is playing with her stuffed animals in her bedroom."

I nodded and decided to just sit and enjoy my coffee without my monkey climbing all over me. "So what's on your agenda for the day?"

"I'm going to go home, take a nap, then head out to a sports bar to find a man to warm my bed. Hell, maybe two of them."

I lifted my coffee mug and held it up.

Christine clinked hers to mine.

"Best of luck, my friend." She deserved to get what she desired after the evening she'd bought for me.

Completely relaxed, still feeling thoroughly sated, and wanting to just curl up on the couch and snuggle, I said goodbye to Christine and went in search of my bossy-boo.

Her face lit up when she saw me in her doorway, and she flew at me with a silly shriek.

I swept my daughter up into my arms and held her tight, breathing in the scent of cheap baby wash Christine must have used the night before to bathe her. My heart swelled with love, but a slight pang radiated through my chest.

It had been delicious having a man's hands on my body again.

Too bad the guy who had seemed interested in me as a person had proven to be a gentleman but wasn't available for me to truly think about outside memories and future fantasies.

I wondered if he would remember the single mom who had unloaded the shit of her past into his ears in the first half-hour of her paid-for date, but I reminded myself I'd been a blip on his radar.

There one night, gone the next.

Such was the life of a paid escort, and it would be best for me to keep that in the forefront of my mind so I didn't start dreaming about the unattainable.

Chapter 11

Reid

For the first time in what felt like forever, all the guys met up Saturday night for beer and burgers. Wren had made plans with her co-worker from the pharmacy, so Blake sat beside me, already three drinks in and grinning. Colton had sent Hudson and Madeline out for a dinner date on their own, and Micah didn't have a woman, same as me.

I should have been ecstatic to get to hang with my friends. Instead, I slouched, toying with the damp label on my beer bottle.

"What's up your ass?" Blake asked me.

"Nothing," Colton replied for me with a snicker, "but if you need a dick..." He waggled his eyebrows at me.

"Fuck off," I muttered, backhanding the jerk. "You bring that thing near me, and I'll tell Hudson. He'll bend you over his knee and redden your ass for sure."

"Fuck yeah," he said with an exaggerated groan. "I love it when my man's hands make me squirm on his lap."

I envied the light in Colton's eyes even though I didn't understand the draw to men or pain. To each his own, but that glow of happiness, of contentment on his face, he'd felt after having found love radiated to anyone who looked at him.

He and Blake were lucky bastards.

"How are things with your mommy and daddy?" I asked Colton, wanting to rile him up the same way he enjoyed doing to me.

He smirked, sipped his beer, and set it down on the high table without a hard clink out of annoyance I'd been hoping for.

"They're fucking awesome," he replied and leaned forward, crossing his arms, his dark eyes full of mischief. "How's the single life?" he tossed back at me, poking the bear as always.

If it had been a couple of days earlier, I would have said spectacular, but shit had changed within the previous twenty-four hours. I still couldn't get out of my funk that had all started the second I'd laid eyes on Jessica Lindy. Then hearing about her little mini-me...how could the thought of another man's child in Jessie's arms make me want her even more?

I didn't have a contract with Elite until the following weekend, but that didn't stop my stomach from churning over the thought of sticking my dick into another woman's body.

One day at a time, I'd told myself pretty much nonstop since walking out of that hotel room, trying not to think about how I would handle my next clients of Elite's.

I shifted and glanced at Micah who studied me. A quick twist of my neck sent my focus over to the bar where I would usually look for someone to talk into sitting on my cock once our guy's night out ended. Not a single one of the women interested me. There was no desperate draw, no hint of arousal, even by the blonde with the big tits glancing my way with a coy smirk on her painted lips.

Jessie had wiped her lipstick off within seconds of sitting down at the restaurant, her grimace over the stained napkin suggesting she disliked the stuff as much as I did.

She'd been sweet on my tongue when I'd held her in my arms, her whimpers like gasoline to the flames of lust that had brewed in my groin all throughout our date. I should have at least gone for another taste while pleasuring her with my fingers. Maybe then she'd have given in to the crazy energy between us.

"If I didn't know any better," Blake said to me, "I'd say you need to get laid. Didn't you work for your pimp last night?"

Micah's stare continued to tingle my face. "Reid had his first single client," he said. "How was she?" he asked me. "Jessica, right?"

I glanced at my night boss and nodded.

"Did you fuck her?" Blake asked, and I sipped my beer, once more back in that hotel room, hearing her whimpers, her cries of release I'd lusted to swallow down.

"No. She didn't want it."

Colton let out a fake gasp. "A woman paid for your cock —then *didn't want it?* Did you forget to manscape, or did you have trouble getting it up for the poor woman?"

"Fuck off," I muttered again, tossing one of the fries I had leftover on my plate at his face.

Chuckling, he swatted it away.

I threw a second, and it hit him smack between the eyes. "Ha!"

"Asshole," he muttered, grabbing a napkin to wipe the grease off his forehead.

"Children," Micah chided, and everyone but me laughed.

"Seriously, Reid, what the fuck is going on?" Blake asked, his brow furrowing.

We hadn't been on the jobsite that day, so I hadn't seen him since my date with Jessie. Otherwise, I would have already spilled the beans.

"That woman..." I shook my head, at a loss for words since I couldn't decide *what* she'd done to me or how.

"Someone is smitten," Colton suggested.

"Am not," I muttered.

"Shit." Blake studied me just as hard as Micah.

I blew out a heavy exhale and sat back in my chair, palms on my thighs, still clueless on what to say.

Micah kept silent, but I could still feel his cool stare.

"You gonna see her again?" Colton asked, the only one at our table seemingly unaffected by my somberness.

"I left my cell number on the back of my card." It hurt to glance up at Micah to get a read on his face about what I'd done with one of my cards he'd provided. He didn't appear moved by the fact I would offer myself to the woman again without him being the middleman who would benefit. "I'm not really sure why," I tried to explain. "She's in no place to trust a man. Hell, she wouldn't even let me fuck her even though her friend had paid for my dick."

"If she just needed a night without responsibilities and you made that happen, then there's nothing to feel bad about," Micah said. "Your job is to please my clients. If that's having good conversation and tucking them into their hotel bed without sex, then that's what you do."

Oh, we'd definitely had some form of sex, but I treasured what Jessie had gifted me too damn much to share what she'd allowed me to do to her body with the guys.

"So what's the game plan?" Blake asked.

"I don't have one," I replied. "Not unless Jessie calls me."

But even then, I wasn't sure what I actually wanted from the woman. While there was definitely attraction and I got damn butterflies whenever I thought too long on her, I was an escort with trust issues. She was a single mom who wasn't interested in my dick or getting involved with another man.

"Three months," Colton tossed out, pulling my gaze off my beer bottle.

"One week," Blake stated firmly.

I glanced between the two of them, hating their knowing smirks. "The fuck, guys?"

Colton got all up in my face, his growing grin obnoxious as hell. "Your world is about to turn upside down, my friend." He clasped my shoulder and squeezed hard.

I straightened, the hairs on my nape rising like Colton had made a prophecy or some such shit, something I wouldn't be able to stop...like a speeding train set on crashing into me. "What's that supposed to mean?" I asked, hesitant because I wasn't sure I wanted to hear what he had to say.

Colton smirked and glanced over at Blake who returned his knowing look.

The fuckers were taking too much goddamned joy out of my strange suffering.

"*I'm not smitten*," I reiterated what Colton had implied a second earlier. "I'm not." I sure as hell felt like it though. And what did that mean for my immediate future? My night job?

"Micah?" I gave him my full attention, needing some

guidance. I couldn't quit because I had the hots for a single mom I wouldn't allow myself to fully fall for.

He stared me down without a trace of a smile. "Do what you have to, Sullivan."

Did he think I was just going to up and leave Elite? Drop my night job because my thoughts were simply tangled up?

I didn't want to get involved with another woman after the knifing Tara had done to me. Couldn't fucking handle the stress already tensing my shoulders over the prospect of allowing a person that deep into my heart again.

"I'm not going to go quitting on you because of some beautiful blonde who has a kid and doesn't want another dick near her body," I finally stated firmly, believing that speaking the words would make my stomach unclench.

She hadn't shied away from my hard length against her thigh though. Had I pushed for more, would she have given her body to me?

"Fuck." I sagged in my chair.

"You're right, Blake," Colton said with a nod, still smirking at me. "I give the man a week."

Groaning, I rubbed a hand over my face. "Can we change the subject? Please?"

"I'm building myself a new house," Micah said, and that drew Blake and Colton's full focus off me and my issues.

If only my own mind could be so easily swayed to a topic other than Jessica Lindy and the curveball she'd thrown at me.

Chapter 12

Jessica

I blew a wayward hair out of my eyes and reached into the toilet, a sponge clutched in my rubber-gloved hand. The final chore of my Saturday morning before sitting down to my bills and a near-worthless checkbook.

The Blue's Clues theme song drifted in through the bathroom door. I'd left Cassie on her secondhand Dora chair, a plastic cup of fishies in hand while I finished scrubbing the bathroom.

Heaving a sigh, I allowed la-la land to take over my mind as I'd done all week long since my mommy's night out. It had been eight days since my date with Reid, too many hours to calculate since I'd climaxed from his fingers alone, but I couldn't stop thinking about him.

A shiver rippled over my skin, making goosebumps rise along my arms.

While Reid hadn't pushed for full-on sex, he'd more than given me a taste of what I was missing. The hard length of him that had pressed against me while he'd been massaging my back would have felt ten times better than his thick fingers reaching deep inside me too.

Heat flushed through me, and even though I squatted, elbow-deep in a toilet bowl, I considered getting myself off again. I'd never masturbated so much in my life. Even when Devon and I had first started fooling around, I'd never been so horny, my body weeping for penetration at all hours of the day.

I should have slept with Reid. Should have fucked the night away until I couldn't breathe or think. Should have been pleasantly sore in the morning when crawling out of that hotel bed.

Stupid, stupid, stupid.

How many times had I said the same while fingering his business card over the previous week? I hadn't called, nor would I. I couldn't afford Elite Escort's fees—I'd checked their website just because I needed the proof for my fanciful brain full of what-ifs and the few fantasies I'd allowed myself to fill my loneliness.

Why would he want me to contact him, anyway? He got laid a lot. Probably a few times a week with different women. Like Devon, Reid wasn't the type of man a woman could trust with her heart.

"I don't need to be another notch in his belt, thank you very much," I grumbled while wringing out the sponge and tossing it into the bucket beside me.

Maybe he'd left the card because he'd felt like a failure and wanted to hook up for his man-pride since I'd refused a ride on his dick that night.

I flushed the suds down the toilet and stood, hands on my hips, rethinking that last thought.

Reid had seemed like too much of a gentleman for such immaturity. He *had* been a gentleman. A good listener. A free sharer of personal information as though he'd been truly interested in us getting to know one another. A great kisser who had swoon-worthy hands I could not. Get. Off. My. Mind!

"Too bad I didn't meet him on that damn dating site." I yanked off the yellow gloves with a snap, my brow furrowed and stomach all messed up.

"Mah!" Cassie called from the other room, a giggle in her voice. "Mah!"

My heart swelled with joy as it always did when my daughter hollered for me as though desperate to show me something.

She made life worth living, and I would protect her with my last breath from any potential heartbreak if I could. That included bringing a man into her world only to have him walk away when booze or drugs took over because I was too much to handle. Even worse, when Mini-Me proved to be double the trouble from him when I felt she was anything but.

"Man!" She laughed and gibbered something about Blue's friend Magenta.

Smiling, I dropped the gloves and went to see what my precious girl wanted to share with me.

Chapter 13

Reid

I shifted my truck into park and stared at the front door to the LaCroix residence, a sprawling single-story mansion on the ocean. A salt-scented breeze blew in through my opened window, and my mind turned to whiskey-colored eyes and a sweet smile.

Ducking and running had been a shit move.

I should have just jerked off in the bathroom and crawled back into bed with her. Should have pulled her up against me, breathed in her strawberry scent, and enjoyed the fantasy of softening my heart and letting her in for just a few hours longer. Should have taken advantage of every second beside her. Fuck the fact that I didn't want to like her too much, and also fuck the fact I could have fallen for her and ended up with another broken heart.

She'd been my last job of the weekend before, and I hadn't been able to think of much else all week long while working my ass off at the high school construction site. But no matter how much I tired myself out during the day, thoughts of Jessie had kept me up every night.

She hadn't called. I hoped she would, yet I didn't. I

reminded myself of my youngest sister who never knew what she wanted, and when she did finally decide, she always changed her mind a day later. The worst part? I had clients inside waiting for me.

I glanced at the double front doors.

Doc LaCroix enjoyed having control over his submissive pain whore of a wife. He also enjoyed allowing other men to get her off while he sat back and watched. Good thing the missus didn't mind other men giving her pleasure to please her master.

I'd been with them once before, not long after starting with Elite back in January. The wife was a petite blonde with shapely legs and a bare, pink pussy that had me ready to pound away within moments of first seeing her.

"Just pretend Doc's wife is Jessie," I grumbled at my flaccid dick stuffed into my jeans, "and we'll be fine."

Fucker didn't so much as twitch, so I popped a little blue pill since I had to perform even if my cock wasn't in the mood.

Doc opened the door a few minutes later and greeted me with a slight French accent. At five feet and a few inches, Doc looked more like a prepubescent kid than a forty-something neurosurgeon peering up at me. He certainly didn't lack in the confidence department. Even though I towered over him and his scrawny body, the man could hold his own. The quiet, dominant aura about him demanded attention and respect. His slender fingers performed surgery every week, but after seeing the marks he'd left on his wife our first go-round, I decided I would never fuck around with him.

The missus, however, I'd been happy to mess a hell of a lot with last time, allowing the good doc to boss me around like a sex slave. But no pain for me. Hard limit.

As I followed Doc to their basement playroom, I couldn't muster any excitement I would have felt if the appointment had been pre-Jessie.

Goddamnit. Get your head in the game.

Doc LaCroix had tied his wife spread eagle on the bed against the far wall. Red welts crisscrossed her abdomen and thighs. Ropes bound her large breasts to the point they'd begun to turn bluish. Her plump lips wrapped around a ball gag while a black blindfold hid her eyes.

I followed Doc into the room and paused beside him at the foot of the bed, not turned off by their kink but not aroused by it either.

His wife's body, minus the grotesquely squeezed breasts, looked so much like my memory of Jessie that my chest ached.

"Her pleasure has been earned," Doc said, turning toward a leather chair in the dim corner. "Show her what a good pet she's been."

Focusing on the memory of the need in Jessie's eyes and the sounds of her moans while I'd had my hands on her, I tugged off my shirt. I reached for the button on my jeans and paused, my attention far from the job in front of me. How the hell could I fuck another woman when all I could think about was Jessie?

She wasn't anything to me beyond a past client, but her memory stuck with me stronger than any superglue. Her eyes haunted me every hour of the day. Faced with touching another woman, my stomach rebelled, rumbling my guts.

"Can't do it, Doc," I rasped out, grabbing my shirt off the floor and pulling it on. "I'm sorry."

"Is everything okay, young man?" he asked, catching up to me as I climbed the stairs on a mission to get the hell out of there before I puked over their marble floor.

"Yes. I just...can't." I couldn't meet his gaze, even when he clasped me on the shoulder in their vast entryway.

"Shall I reschedule, or would you prefer we ask for another escort to play with us next time?" At least he didn't sound pissed off like some clients would have been.

The muscle in my jaw ticked as I considered his suggestion. Jessie had taken up residence in my head, but what the fuck was I supposed to do with that truth when I had a job to finish? I expected Micah wouldn't be as forgiving as the doc, but I didn't feel I had a choice. Couldn't fucking do it. I swallowed hard. "Perhaps another would be best," I stated, wondering when the fuck, if ever, Jessie would escape my thoughts.

He nodded. "I'll call Elite and let them know."

"No." I held out my hand which he shook. "I'll do it and make sure you're fully refunded for tonight. Next time you utilize Elite's services, it's on me."

I'd let Micah down, but I wasn't about to have him lose a customer over my inability to fuck because my damn emotions had gotten caught up in a petite, blonde single mom.

How the fuck had I gotten ensnared? I'd allowed one little kiss...okay, so not exactly *little*, but I'd known better.

Jessie had just been so damn gorgeous against the city's backdrop in that window. And the chemistry ten times stronger than any magnetic force? She'd drawn me in past the point of caring about consequences.

Forehead dented in a deep frown, I pulled out of the LaCroixs' driveway, the setting sun blinding me briefly with golden warmth I wanted to sink beneath.

Exactly as Jessie had tempted me to do. The second I'd set eyes on her, she'd become more than just a client. More than the promise of money in my pocket.

Micah's customers expected my hard cock and some-times to merely be eye candy for events. He paid me to do whatever was necessary to please the people who trusted him to deliver their heart's desires.

Even if every single word, every touch, and moan were lies on my lips.

Unfortunately, I didn't have it in me to fake shit that night, not when my body refused to perform what I'd been hired to do.

Screw the contract I'd signed with Elite about client privacy.

I needed to see Jessie again.

What I hoped to find out or learn about myself, I had no fucking clue. Pure yearning turned my wheel northward, and I sped up Route 1 to put my newfound obsession to rest once and for all so I could get back to my uncomplicated life.

Chapter 14

Jessica

Exhaustion tugged at my eyelids, and I snuggled my face into Cassie's warm neck, the jingle of another silly cartoon blaring from the TV. She smelled like her lavender nighttime bath wash and her footie nightie like generic dryer sheets. I landed a few smooches on her soft skin before she pushed a hand up to block my lips.

"No way!" she barked, her attention glued to the screen.

I relaxed back onto the couch, allowing my tired muscles the rest they deserved while giving Cassie some space since she preferred it while zoning out with her cartoons.

The apartment around us sparkled and smelled like citrus from my weekly cleaning, allowing me to semi-relax. All I had left to do was to put my daughter down and finally shower the stench off my own body. Then I could indulge in a glass of the cheap wine I'd splurged on and shouldn't have—

A knock sounded on the door, and I stiffened, frowning.

I hadn't buzzed anyone into the building, nor was I expecting company.

It must be one of the neighbors.

Sighing, I slid from beneath Cassie, settling her on the couch with her blankie. "Mommy will be right back."

She ignored me in favor of the little pink pig bossing her little brother around on the TV and didn't so much as blink when I pressed a light kiss to the top of her hair.

I made my way into the kitchen on weary legs and pulled open the door.

Reid stood in the hallway, hands shoved in his jeans' pockets.

My breath left in a rush as heat erupted in my core, flushing through my body.

"Hi," he said, his brown irises twinkling as his lips curled upward.

God, that smile...those eyes. I tightened my grip on the doorknob as his woodsy cologne assaulted my senses and brought my tastebuds to life. Instantaneous humiliation swept over me as I imagined what I looked like in my ratty cleaning clothes, how I smelled after spending the day scrubbing.

"H-how did you get in here without the key code?" I asked, my voice no more than a timid squeak. At least my embarrassment overrode the arousal his appearance had caused so I didn't sound like a needy, breathless dick-starved wonton woman which I totally was.

"I waited for a neighbor to get home from wherever the hell it was they'd gone and snuck in behind them."

His smooth tone erupted butterflies in my belly, but it was the knowledge of him slipping into our secure building that made a shiver slide down my spine and raise the hairs on my neck. I'd chosen that apartment building for its safety. At least I trusted Reid to not have ill intentions toward me or my daughter.

"What are you doing here?" I asked, more than a little unnerved and off-kilter regardless of at least that little bit of trust I had in him.

"I wanted to see you."

I studied his face, unable to catch a trace of dishonesty or bullshit. Hell, he didn't even seem to care that I was a walking disaster. No curl of the lips, no grimace lined his face as he glanced down over me in my near rags for clothing draped over my body.

"Why?"

His smile faded as his gaze once more rested on my face. "I can't get you out of my mind."

"That sounds like a cheesy song lyric," I said, peering up at him, unsure of how to feel or even what to think over his sincere declaration.

"Can I come in?" he asked quietly, coiling need in my core.

"I can't afford you."

His brow drew down, seemingly almost offended by the truth I spoke—but maybe he'd come to regret his choice of profession. "I'm here as plain old me, Jessie, not Elite's man whore extraordinaire. I'm not looking to take your money, and I won't try to get in your panties. I just want...to talk."

He sounded as though he'd meant every word, but I couldn't figure out why he had shown up if it wasn't to obtain what I'd denied him the weekend before.

"I considered calling, you know," I said, keeping my firm stance in the doorway since I wasn't ready to just let him into my safe haven and meet my daughter.

A hint of a smile curved his mouth. "Why didn't you?"

"Because I can't get involved with anyone even just for a good time. My focus is Cassie."

Reid glanced over my shoulder toward the living room

where a new tune blared, his expression hopeful as though wanting to get a peek at the little stinker I'd told him all about.

"And I refuse to take a chance on falling for someone only to have my heart broken again," I concluded, my tone firm even though the attraction between us pushed for me to do the opposite.

Reid's dark eyes focused on me once more. He swallowed hard. "I have no idea what is going on inside me, Jessie, but I can't...perform. I-I had to walk away from an Elite client tonight because all I could think about was you. How easy it was to just sit and talk with you. How your expressive eyes made me want to drown and never resurface." He shifted, vulnerability radiating from his expression, but I refused to swoon regardless of the weakness trying to sag my knees. "I decided I would be bold. Take a risk. See what—" he waved a hand between us "—this is."

I chewed the inside of my cheek as temptation tugged on my heartstrings and the moisture factory inside my core.

"You deserve more, Jessica Lindy," he murmured.

Staring up into his dark eyes sure as hell didn't help the rational side of my brain. Peering into their brown depths tugged on every cell inside me, the secret longings I'd refused to consider for years. Desire to reach out and grasp, to hold close, to wrap myself up in someone else's energy rather than my own lagging strength swept through me. And my body? Every inch of me lusted to once more enjoy what Reid had given me the weekend before.

My inability to deny myself relief from constant stress relented, and my grip on the door handle loosened.

"Mah!" Cassie called from the living room, ripping my focus back on the reality of my life, my responsibilities, and my reason for living.

My throat clogged as disappointment crashed over me, and I once more tightened my grasp, twisting the knob. "I-I can't do this," I whispered with nothing more than a ragged exhale.

"Jessie, wait." Reid put his palm on the door to keep me from closing it in his face as I'd begun to do. "Please."

Cassie came first—her safety would *always* come first. My wants and desires could have no sway over my decisions outside of her. "I can't."

Reid and I stared at each other in silence while my heartbeat pulsed in my ears, and even though a tangible connection extended between us like a wire charged with electricity, I stood stubborn and unmoving.

He exhaled heavily and nodded. "Okay." He took a step back and shoved his hands in his pockets again, never once taking his gaze off my face.

Inner lip between my teeth, I shut the door and leaned against it, tears stinging my eyes. Reid Sullivan had slipped into my life with ease, taking up residence in my mind, but the memory of him would have to be enough for my lonely heart.

Chapter 15

Reid

"Goddamn motherfucking piece of shit!" I tossed my jammed nail gun aside.

"The fuck is your problem?" Blake asked, sunlight glinting off his shades as he ambled toward me.

I'd been too worked up to be an office prop and had made myself busy with the other guys framing out a section of the new school. But no matter what I did, it seemed life was out to fuck me up.

"Goddamn piece of shit," I said again while motioning toward the gun with my chin.

Blake chuckled while I grabbed my cold Dunks cup off the cement floor and guzzled down the last of my morning's coffee. "Jessie, huh?" he asked.

I nodded, my guts clenched up over the fact I couldn't get past her. "Can't sleep without dreaming about her. Can't get it up because of her too. Took fucking pills to make that shit happen with Micah's clients over the weekend, but my head wasn't in the game. I had to fucking cancel. Twice."

Blake didn't offer a comment or snicker like I'd expected

after the shit he and Colton had given me over being smitten.

I threw my empty Dunks cup toward a barrel and snatched up the nail gun. It took me a few seconds, but I pried the jammed nail loose and got it working again.

"So what are you going to do about it?" Blake asked once I shot a few nails into place.

"Nothing I *can* do about it." It wasn't like I was interested in more than a few rounds with the gorgeous blonde… or was I? "Fuck." I rolled my head, stretching out my neck. "*Should* I do anything about it?" I asked, glancing over at him.

He eyed the two-by-four I'd just nailed into place. "I think you need to put this shit to rest in your head one way or another so you can get back to work."

I glowered at Blake.

"You like her?" he asked, turning toward me.

That, at least, was an easy answer. "Yeah."

"Is she pulling on you like an inescapable tractor beam and resistance seems futile?"

I snickered. "You're showing your inner Trekkie."

"You were a closet geek up until last year too, you prick." He elbowed me.

"Wren was good for something," I teased even though I didn't feel the least bit in the mood for joking around.

"She's the best."

Fuck, how I envied that happiness in Blake's eyes, the sated bliss in his voice as he'd spoken those words. He'd been a playboy since high school, refusing to ever settle down, but he'd gotten lucky with Wren, the same as Colton had with the Youngs.

Was it possible I could find something similar after how Tara had broken my heart?

I shuddered at the memory of how I'd laid in bed for days and the tears I'd cried over my ex-fiancée. Sure, the pain had lessened a bit, but would it ever dissolve to the point I would consider putting my heart out there again where I might get crushed?

And if I couldn't allow myself to be vulnerable, was being an escort all I had left to look forward to?

No exchange of vows I *knew* could be kept thanks to watching my family find their happily ever afters. No picket fences and little rug rats climbing all over me I dreamed of having like my nieces and nephews. No one beside me as I grew all old and wrinkly, my joints aching for rest.

Did I want to be alone for the rest of my life? Merely uncle and son until I drew my last breath?

"You want to see her again, but you're scared shitless. Am I right?" Blake asked.

"Pretty much."

He shrugged like Tara shredding my heart and bleeding me out was no big deal. "So give it a shot. Hound the shit outta Jessie like I did with Wren. She relented, and I found my forever girl."

Slowly releasing a heavy exhale, I turned back to the stud I'd nailed into place. The thing was crooked as fuck. I pulled the hammer off my belt and hit the bottom to level it out. If only my thoughts could be so easily aligned. "My situation is a little more complicated."

"Because of the kid?"

"And the fact that Jessie's ex hurt her to the point where she doesn't trust anyone, doesn't let anyone past her walls."

"Sucks for you."

Finding the stud straight enough, I glanced over at my friend. "Tell me something I *don't* know," I muttered.

"I proposed to Wren."

The nail gun slipped from my left hand and clanged on the floor. Shoving my hammer back into its hook on my tool belt, I turned to face him fully, hands on my hips. "What?"

A sheepish grin flashed his pearly whites. "We're getting married in September."

Happiness and envy shot through me in equal measure. "No shit."

"Yep. And I want you to be my best man."

I pulled him into a back-slapping man-hug, my smile genuine even though heaviness settled in my chest over what I'd lost. "Congrats, Harper, and yeah, I'll fucking stand beside you."

"Thanks." We stepped apart, both of us grinning like a couple of fools. "If you think Jessie might be it for you," Blake said, clasping my shoulder, "don't give up. Find ways to let her know you're thinking about her—that you care. Maybe you'll get lucky in love for a change like I did, and she can be your plus one when Wren and I finally tie the knot."

Long after Blake ambled off, I considered his words, my thoughts, and the possibilities.

Although scared shitless didn't begin to describe the feelings inside me over pursuing some sort of relationship again, I allowed myself to hope. I longed for what Blake had found. What my parents and sisters had as well.

Jessie had shut me out, but like Blake, I decided another attempt at breaking down her walls would be worth the effort. Even if she turned me down, at least I would be able to say I'd tried.

JF

"Gemberling Insurance," a soft, feminine voice said. "How may I direct your call?"

"Is Christine available?" I asked, grabbing my lunch cooler out of my truck's cab.

"One moment, please."

I wasn't sure how to approach the coming conversation. Christine knew who I was, remembered me from high school, or so Jessie had told me over dinner, but could she be schmoozed into giving me what I wanted?

"This is Christine."

I recognized the smooth, sexy tone from years past, but it didn't do anything for my limp dick like it would have done pre-Jessie. "Hey, Chris. This is Reid Sullivan."

"How can I help you, Mr. Sull—" She coughed. "Wait. *Sully?*"

"One and the same," I said, grimacing at hearing my childhood nickname Blake was the only one I allowed to use it when addressing me.

Her chuckle came through loud and clear over the line. "How the hell are ya?"

I hadn't called her to play sly fox, so I went with the straight-up truth. If she was anything like the no-nonsense girl she'd been back in high school, she would appreciate me being candid.

"I'm not sleeping worth a shit, and it's all your fault," I stated, uncaring of how petulant I sounded.

Her barked laughter made my forehead dent in a deep frown. "How's that my fault?"

"I met your little friend, and now I can't think about anyone or anything else." I sat on my tailgate and propped open my lunchbox lid.

"That sounds like a *you* problem," Christine pretty

much purred in my ear as though thoroughly enjoying my misery.

"She shared over our dinner that you two are pretty close, so I'm expecting you know I showed up at her place last weekend?" I dug my ham sandwich from my cooler.

"She also told me that she shut the door in your face." Christine almost sounded disappointed by that fact.

"Do I have any chance at all?" Silence met my ear for a few seconds.

"Well," Christine finally said, her voice low and muffled. "Jessie has been daydreaming between calls and customers. I'm pretty sure with how she's constantly talking about you that she's as equally enamored."

Light flutters woke inside my chest as I stared at the sandwich in my hand. "Really?"

"I'd bet money on it."

"What'll it take for you to give me her number?" I blurted out the reason for my call.

"Hmm." I swear I could hear the gears turning in Christine's brain. "What's that information worth to you?"

"More than I can pay," I admitted, realizing as I spoke the words how true they were. I needed an in.

"How well do you know your co-worker Jarod?"

I huffed laughter through my nose. Some things and people never changed. "Not good enough to talk him into your bed for free," I told Christine, "but I'll gladly dish out the cash for an evening of his time if that's what you're fantasizing about."

"*God*, yes. I didn't mind hiring you for Jessie, but I draw a line at paying for dick when I can get it easily for free." Her confidence drew a chuckle from me.

I pulled my sandwich from its baggie, finally ready to

eat. "So no one has shackled you to a ball and chain yet, huh?"

"Hell no. Too many flavors to choose from and not enough time to sample them all."

Yep. Christine Gemberling hadn't changed a bit since high school. "So, for one night with Jarod, I get Jessie's number," I clarified and bit into my sandwich.

"Serve up that pretty boy on a hot platter, and I'll pretty much do whatever the hell you want, Sully. Hurt Jessie, though, and I'll carve your testicles out with a dull blade."

My knees inadvertently pressed together, and I choked on the food I'd attempted to swallow. "Still a tough bitch, I see," I rasped and coughed to clear my throat.

"Tough enough to inflict serious damage if you screw this up with her."

I sobered, fearing my own broken heart more than hurting Jessie. "I'm going to try like hell not to."

"You know she isn't quick to trust."

"Yes."

"You also know you have your work cut out for you."

Again, Christine didn't ask a question, but I replied with an affirmative.

"If you're still the sweetheart you were back in the day," Christine stated with a smile in her voice, "I do think you have a shot. And that's the *only* reason I'm breaking Jessie's trust."

I grinned. "A sweetheart...that's why you wouldn't sleep with me in high school, isn't it? I wasn't edgy enough for you."

Christine didn't answer right away, and when she finally did, her tone lacked the assertive boldness she'd had throughout our conversation. "You had 'forever' stamped all over you even in middle school, Sully. That's something I've never been interested in, but Jessie is whether she wants to admit it or not. That girl needs a good, solid man in her life, a partner to share the burdens she carries around like a goddamn cross."

The idea of holding Jessie, offering myself to help see her through life flooded me with a deep yearning I'd never felt before, even with Tara.

I'd fallen hard and fast for Jessie, and even if she wasn't ready to let me in, my days of being a professional third wheel were over.

Chapter 16

Jessica

On the weekends, I might get a dinging text notification or two, but during the week while at work? Hardly ever since the only woman to poke at me sat behind my desk and talked aloud to me whenever she wanted.

I finished up a call for a quote I'd been going through, hopeful the potential client would be in the following day as they'd promised, and pulled off my headset.

I grabbed my purse from beneath my desk and swiped my cell's screen to life. I didn't recognize the number but didn't need to. The typed words shouted loud and clear who had texted me.

I had a dream about beautiful, haunted eyes last night.

Tingles of warmth swept through me, and I smiled. So much for that stubborn stance. How the hell did he weasel his way into my emotions so quickly?

A glance up revealed no one paying attention to me, so I quickly turned my phone's volume to silent and replied, **How did you get my number?**

Reid: **Easy enough to do when you know where to look.**

The pleasant buoyancy of my mood flattened, and my smile faded. I kept my cell number private out of fear Devon would somehow get ahold of it.

My fingers shook as I quickly typed out, **Seriously, how did you get my number? I keep a tight hold on personal info because of my ex.**

I chewed on the inside of my lip while waiting for Reid's reply.

Reid: **I went out on a limb, took a chance, and bribed a little birdie into telling me.**

The only person we both knew...

I shot a glare at the woman sitting at the desk behind mine. Christine chatted into her headset, oblivious to my stare on her flaming red hair.

Huffing an annoyed snort, I turned back around.

Me: **My only friend betrayed me.**

Reid: **I'd like to think WE are friends.**

Friends. With a professional escort. Yet still a man who knew how to listen without telling me his opinions or how to fix my life. Not exactly buddies, but he *had* offered to be of service in more ways than just finding sexual release.

Me: **You did say you were the kind of person that was good to have in a back pocket.**

Reid: **So you still have my card?**

Warmth heated my face. The damn thing sat on my bed stand, a daily reminder of the best night of my life. Not that I would ever tell Reid that.

Me: **It's stuffed in my purse somewhere.**

Reid: **Well, I won't keep you from work. Just**

was thinking about you and wanted you to know.

My fingers flew in response before I gave my reply a second thought. **What was the dream about?**

It took a few for his next text to come through, and once more, I found myself chewing on the inside of my lip, warmth radiating through my core.

Reid: **I sat in the front row of an auditorium and listened to a whiskey-eyed woman give a lecture on parenting. She had a big grin on her face, and the love in her eyes while talking about her Mini-Me made my chest ache.**

I sat back in my chair and stared at his words. Not what I expected *at all*. I had no clue how to reply, and he sent another before my brain moved.

Reid: **I was crushing on your passion for being a mom but woke up before I could tell you so. Figured I'd do it by text once I had enough coffee in me to think straight.**

My smile returned, and I shook my head, sure he lied.

Me: **I don't think I've ever had it bad for someone's mind before.**

Reid's reply was an emoji with hearts for eyes.

Me: **Pretty sure you're full of shit...and I have to get back to work.**

I hit "send" and dropped my phone into my purse, unsure which thoughts to focus on—giddiness or the glass-half-empty ideas my mind usually focused on to keep me and Cassie safe.

The second Christine's call ended, I spun my chair fully around to face her. "You!" I whisper-hollered.

One of her eyebrows arched as she peered at me over

the half-wall shutting her off from the rest of the room. "What about me?"

"You gave Reid my number?"

"In exchange for a night with the original tall, dark, and handsome," she admitted without a hint of regret in her voice or in her glinting, knowing eyes.

I glared even though I wasn't exactly angry. "You gave up private information for dick?" I hissed, keeping my voice down so the other Gemberling employees wouldn't hear our exchange.

"Hopefully, a delicious one." Christine winked, and I rolled my eyes.

"*Seriously?*"

Fucking was her favorite topic alongside sports I could care less about and the need to drop those ten pounds. With no money troubles or family issues, her life allowed for frivolous things to sate her horniness. She didn't have a child to provide for or keep safe, which gave her the ability to focus all her energy on herself.

Envy often hit me when I thought of how easy Christine had it, but Cassie's precious little face flashed in my mind's eye, and I realized once again I wouldn't trade what I had for the chance to be single and carefree again.

Christine's face smoothed out, turning serious. "Reid is a good guy, Jessie. He always has been. I know you're scared of lowering your walls, that you feel you can't trust ever again, but don't you want more? Someone to hold you? Kiss you goodnight and good morning? A man who will help you carry your burdens and Cassie can call daddy?"

Sudden thickness took over my throat, prohibiting me from swallowing or speaking. I'd never shared my deep longings with Christine, but I guessed I hadn't hidden them all that well, same as I'd never been able to shut down my facial expressions from Devon.

"I want all of those more than anything," I choked out. Emotional exhaustion atop finally admitting my desires aloud sagged me into my chair. "I'm so tired of doing everything by myself. Tired of struggling to pay the bills. Tired of going to bed alone and hugging a pillow instead of sharing body heat. It's just so hard to trust."

She smiled kindly. "You won't find your person unless you choose to give someone a chance. Make an attempt at changing your life. Do something out of the ordinary and enjoy getting to know Reid. And if he hurts you, he's well aware I have a knife ready to lob off his balls."

I snorted a laugh, quickly smothering it with my palm.

"Seriously, Jessie," she urged, leaning forward, her eyes intense and filled with hope for me. "You're the forever type —so is he. I'm not interested in happily ever afters, but you should totally go for it."

So easily stated.

Not so easily done.

But how? Reid's interest had already been won, but how did one move forward or even start a conversation?

Hey, I want to take a chance on you but I'm an emotional mess with a shit ton of baggage. What do you say?

Snorting, I turned back to my desk.

I'm looking for a daddy for my kid, someone to help me not fail at life.

Talk about needy. What man wanted a premade family? Especially a guy like Reid who was hot as hell, young, and had pussy land in his inbox without any effort on his part?

He'd seemed sincere, but seriously...

I just couldn't grasp or believe his supposed interest.

Pushing my conflicted thoughts aside, I finished getting the paperwork ready for my ten o'clock appointment. They planned to sign up with Gemberling Insurance for a bundled deal, which would land me a little extra cash for the week.

One bill down.

About twenty others still to pay...

Chapter 17

Reid

I'd gone through Elite's secretary Dina to get the LaCroix fee refunded as well as a credit added for when they requested another escort for an upcoming evening. Unsure how Micah would react to what I'd done—and what I planned to do in dropping my night job—I put off calling him directly.

We'd been friends for years, and I didn't want to disappoint him.

Blake assured me Micah wouldn't give a fuck if I quit, that he'd just hire someone else, but fuck, how I hated letting people down.

Monday night after work, I got in touch with Jarod, thinking he would at least maybe understand what I was going through. While he loved working for Elite, I wondered if he'd been interested in a woman enough it hindered his ability to please customers...or if he'd ever considered tossing in the towel on sure pussy.

"What's up, Sullivan?" he answered.

"Hey, Jarod. Got a minute?" I sprawled out on my couch, eyes closed, free hand scratching at my abs.

"Just finished at the gym and I'm on my way home, so yeah. What's going on?"

I blew out a heavy exhale. "There's this girl…"

He snickered. "You're smitten and want to quit EE."

"Fuck."

"Been there. Done that. Failed and crawled back to Micah."

Rubbing a hand down over my face, I cursed again. "Was he pissed you quit?"

"Nope, and that fact made me feel like a replaceable piece of shit."

"He's a cold-hearted prick," I muttered even though I loved the bastard.

"Nah," Jarod disagreed. "He's just a good businessman who doesn't get his emotions involved with work."

Jarod didn't lie.

"Well, there's more to the story," I said.

"Spill. Like I said, I've got the time."

I told Jarod about Tara. How I'd fallen hard and fast, how I'd dreamed about forever and had taken steps toward building a future with her. Then how she'd tossed it all away for some other guy's dick.

"And you became a professional third wheel after bringing another guy into your bed crushed your heart?" he asked, sounding surprised by the choice I'd made.

"Yeah, I know what I did doesn't make much sense, but at the time, I felt like that's all I was good for. An extra. A side dish but not the main course. Who the fuck knows. Maybe I went that route to further wallow in my misery."

"Fucking sadist."

"Sounds that way, doesn't it?" I asked with a wry tone.

"So this woman Jessie. She was your one-on-one a

couple of weeks ago, right? The client you took on since I was sick?"

"Yep." That reminded me that I needed to let him in on the fact I would be buying a night with him in the near future too.

"So what are you hoping for by sharing all this, Sullivan? Encouragement to go for it? Someone to hold your hand while you tell Micah you're done fucking for money?"

"Shit—neither. Guess I'm just wanting to pick your brain since you're an Elite too. What would you do in my situation?"

"Since you're a great guy who I never could have imagined being an escort if you weren't, I think you need to follow your heart. If Jessie is what you want, then let Micah know the truth. He's not going to be mad. And if shit doesn't work out with Jessie, then come on back to the fold. You're one hell of a partner for those clients who want double the tall, dark, and handsome."

I chuckled along with him. "There's one other thing."

Jarod didn't speak for a second. "Now why the fuck are the hairs on my neck suddenly standing on end?"

Barking out a laugh, I pushed upright and leaned my elbows onto my knees. "I managed to get Jessie's phone number from the woman who had hired an Elite for her."

"Okay..."

"But it cost me."

"The fuck did you do?" Jarod asked, but at least he laughed.

"I promised to pay for a night with you."

"So, what's the problem?"

"There isn't one, but I know the woman. I went to high school with her, and we ran across each other here and there the first couple of years after graduating."

"Your tone and hesitation sound like there's a catch or some shit."

There definitely was. "The woman is an independent, cock-hungry bitch."

"And?"

"She's a fiery redhead with a sensual mouth and rocking body."

"Again, I'm not seeing the issue," Jarod said.

The problem was I could totally see him falling for her, same as every guy she'd gotten into bed back in the day. I couldn't imagine her potency had lessened as she grew older and learned her way around a man's body.

"Just...be careful, alright? She's your type and a major heartbreaker," I warned.

"I don't have a heart to break."

"Yeah, and I didn't think I had much of one left for Jessie to hurt either, but I somehow got my emotions entangled up with the idea of her, and I already know if she turns me down again, it's gonna fucking knife me."

"I'm sorry."

"I'm not." I realized as I stated those words that I had zero regrets over what had gone down with Tara. She'd revealed her disloyalty, and better I had learned the truth of her before tying myself to her legally.

"So when do I get the pleasure of slamming a headboard with this redhead you think is going to eat me alive?"

"When's your next available night?"

"I'm pretty sure my schedule is packed for the upcoming couple of months. You'll have to check in with Dina."

We said our goodbyes, and I hung up, feeling only slightly better than before I'd called Jarod.

Like him, I was booked for the upcoming weekend. If I got a solid no from Jessie about her interest in lowering her walls before Friday, I wouldn't have to quit Elite.

Rubbing a hand down over my face at the thought of her telling me no again, I groaned. Even with pills, even with Jessie denying us a chance to pursue something, I wasn't interested in other women. Money or not.

"Fuck."

I hopped up and headed into my kitchen. Anxiety churned my stomach, but I was hangry as fuck. Over dinner, I would make a plan then set about tackling the barriers Jessie had built around her and Cassie to keep them both safe.

The more I considered the fortress they hid behind, the more I realized the futility of scaling the barriers. Even if she agreed to being friends with me, it could be months until she believed I genuinely wanted more with her, never mind earning her trust.

No fucking way could I weasel my way into their lives before Friday.

Maybe I could take a break from Elite. Not outright quit but let Micah know what I was going through.

I put a call through to Dina first, leaving a message she would get in the morning to reassign my clients for Friday and Saturday night. Then I shot off a text to Micah asking if he had time to talk.

He didn't text back, simply called.

"Sullivan," he said by way of greeting, his tone stern yet bland—unfeeling—as usual.

"Hey." I swallowed hard, suddenly unsure of the decision I'd made. "So, um...there's this girl."

His heavy exhale sounded loud as fuck in my ear. "The

same one Blake and Colton were giving you shit about the last time we went out? The beautiful blonde who has a kid and didn't want a dick near her body?"

Almost verbatim what I'd told him that night. "Yeah."

"Is she the reason you dropped both clients last weekend?"

Fuck. I slammed my eyelids shut. "Yeah. Sorry. I should have gotten in touch with you before now, but I didn't want to piss you off."

"Why would I be upset? Quit if you want. Take a hiatus. Doesn't matter to me. I've actually got a couple of guys interested in signing with Elite."

I was replaceable regardless of my friendship with Micah...just like Jarod had said.

That fact definitely stung my ego.

"I need a break for now," I stated, keeping the door open in the event Jessie turned me down for good and I somehow found a way to think about attempting to pleasure other women.

"Not a problem. I'll let Dina know to toss you to the back burner. But, Sullivan?"

"Hmm?"

"I hope she's the one." His tone held sincerity.

I sagged. "Thanks, man. I'm scared as fuck, but I'm hoping so too. Just gotta tear down those walls she built to keep her and Cassie safe."

"Good luck."

Fuck knew I would need it.

But at least I no longer had an exact deadline. If it took me as long as it had Blake to obtain his Wren, I didn't care. I would focus on the pot of gold at the end of the Jessie rainbow while making her comfortable with my presence in her life.

Maybe I'd get lucky enough to be a third wheel of a different sort...one in her little family of two.

Chapter 18

Jessica

I burrowed under my blankets, tattered paperback in hand, when my cell dinged a text notification. A shot of adrenaline sped my heartbeat as I grabbed it off my bedside table.

Reid: ***poke poke* You still awake?**

Warm tingles raced over my skin. I'd been burdened all day over Christine's push to do something I feared. Choosing outside my comfort zone to get to know Reid a little better to see what exactly his intentions were.

I didn't have the drive to pursue, wasn't sure I wanted to rock my life's boat enough to reach out to him. I'd figured that if he was truly interested, felt a serious draw, he wouldn't give up so easily.

He'd taken a second first step after I'd shut my door in his face by texting me at work.

I could appreciate persistence.

Me: **Unfortunately, yes.**

I bit the inside of my lip, waiting.

Reid: **I can't sleep.**

Snuggling under my blankets, I smiled and texted back, fully intending to fish. **How come?**

Reid: **Can't stop thinking about you.**

Heat rushed through, and I rubbed my thighs together, luxuriating in the sweet burn memories of him never failed to simmer inside me.

Me: **More lectures?**

Reid: **Not when I can control my DAY dreams**.

His wink emoji didn't have the same twinkling eyes I expected he did in that moment of flirting. Longing crashed over me, intensifying my arousal, but thoughts of emotional cost still screamed in the back of my mind.

I texted back an eye-rolling emoji rather than give in to the conversation he obviously hoped to have.

Reid: ***knife in my heart* How was the rest of your day?**

I read his text three times, unsure what to think over his about-face in changing the topic when I'd expected more flirting or at least sexual innuendos. Deciding to go with the flow, I texted back, **Decent. I signed two new clients, which means I'll almost be caught up with my bills by the end of next week when I get paid.**

Reid: **That's great!**

Me: **Then I got another silent call yesterday. Probably Devon.**

Reid replied with a scowling face, then asked about Cassie.

My heart a puddle of goo, I smiled and settled in to text him all about the picture I'd hung on the fridge. She'd drawn two images in school she'd claimed to be ice cream and kitties. He asked to see them, so I actually got out of bed and took a shot of them hanging side by side.

His laughter emojis widened my smile.

JB

Reid and I chatted on and off over the next two weeks—by text during the day and phone calls late into the night. He didn't pursue hooking up again and kept our conversations on lighter topics.

Even though I hadn't seen him since that night I'd shut the door in his face, I honestly felt I knew him better than my own mother. He showed more interest in my life than she ever had.

Every conversation began with him asking me about my day and how Cassie was doing.

I went on and on about my little stinker finally deciding she didn't have to use a pacifier anymore and how she'd eaten oatmeal without coercion. Every milestone excited him just as much as they did me. It seemed like he gained pleasure from her antics, the daily growth of her becoming her own little person.

Snuggling with Cassie on the couch for her nightly routine of snacks and cartoons, I kept my eye on my cell, waiting for Reid to reach out like he always did after a long day's work.

Butterflies raced in my belly as the minutes passed. I'd come to look forward to our interactions, loved laughing over his stories about his childhood with three sisters and the rug rats that had made him an uncle.

Even in texts, I could tell the man hoped for a family of his own, and Christine's constant assurance that she'd only ever known him to be a complete doll had begun to ease my doubts and hesitation.

But I wouldn't push for more no matter how much my

body wished for and dreamed of it. What we'd grown in the days following him showing up unannounced at my house was something different. Rare. Budding friendship without allowing lust to muddy waters.

Hope bloomed and along with it, a real desire for more than friendship.

A shot of adrenaline kicked through me at my phone's notification ding.

Reid: **I got Cassie a present for using the big girl potty for the first time yesterday.**

A gift meant he planned on seeing us. Smiling and trying—and failing—to rid my belly of butterflies, I texted back, **You didn't have to do that.**

Reid: **Wanted to. Can I stop by?**

There it was. The opportunity to take the next step. Surprisingly, no trace of fear worried its way through my brain. I wanted to see him. Blowing out a slow exhale, I made the choice to open a metaphorical door into my life while still keeping Cassie physically out of the picture.

Me: **How bout I meet you somewhere tomorrow?**

Reid: **Too late.**

A knock sounded, and I yelped, flinching.

"Mah!" Cassie growled at me for disturbing her. "Phia!" she exclaimed, pointing at the screen and the princess in purple she adored.

"Sorry," I murmured, my pulse racing as I weaseled from beneath her. "Gotta get the door."

Like the last time Reid had shown up uninvited, I looked like shit in my ripped sweats and stretched sweatshirt.

At least I'd showered and didn't smell like sweat and

cleaning products.

Still, I stomped across the kitchen and yanked the door open, trying for a glare at being put on the spot without having the chance to make myself at least somewhat pretty.

"Hi." He grinned, the warmth in his eyes sucking me in like a melted frap through a straw on a hot summer day.

One hand propped on my hip, I pretended to glare up at him. "How did you get in my building?"

"Same as a couple of weeks ago—waited for a neighbor to get home."

"Didn't trust me to let you in?" I raised an eyebrow.

"I'll admit to questioning your stubbornness, yeah." He shrugged, not appearing the least bit contrite over sneaking his way inside.

And his sheepish grin?

Pure life to the butterflies and warmth in my belly.

I glanced at the purple gift bag with glitter tissue paper in his hand, any resolve to keep him at arm's length dissolving. "You really didn't have to do that."

Reid handed the gift to me, and I fought the need to press my thighs together as our fingers brushed in the exchange. "I'm a firm believer in rewarding people—kids and adults alike—for taking big steps."

His wink and the curl of his lips suggested I take a leap forward. *Try.* Give him a chance to prove himself.

My stomach flipped over in the sweetest agony known to womankind and I bit on my lower lip.

"Mah! Phia over!"

I clenched my eyelids shut as little feet pattered close, Sophia's theme song tinkling in the background. With less than a second to make a decision over Reid, I decided not to. Mini-Me meeting someone new, male or female, didn't mean squat unless I allowed it.

Or I could simply leave the choice up to her...

Cassie brushed against the back of my knees, but I still couldn't make myself open my eyes and face the moment. "Mah!" She tugged on my ratty sweats.

I grabbed the waistband with my free hand to keep her from yanking them down.

"Hi there."

Blinking, I found Reid squatting at eye level with my daughter.

"Hi." Cassie beamed at him, uncaring that a complete stranger stood in our doorway. "Phia over," she told him without clinging to my leg like she normally would do when meeting someone new.

"Sophia's over, huh?" he asked with a smile, and that was it.

Reid Sullivan knew who Sophia was to my daughter. He'd paid attention when asking me about her favorite princess.

All tension drained from my body, my eyesight hazing as Cassie nodded.

"Who's your favorite—Crackle or the blue-ribbon bunny?" Reid asked, giving her his full focus again.

"Mimimus."

"I like him too." Reid glanced up at me, that damn twinkle in his eyes over her mispronouncing the pegasus's name. "Who doesn't like purple flying horses?"

Cassie released her hold on my sweats, grabbed Reid's hand, and tugged. "Mah! Move!"

With a sigh, I stepped back and allowed my daughter to tug Reid into what used to be my man-free safe zone.

Plain old Reid Sullivan showed up looking delicious in a tight black T-shirt and ass-hugging jeans, and I was a frumpy, messy-bun disaster. He didn't seem to care about my state while traipsing through the small kitchen into the living room.

I set the gift on the table and followed along after them.

Cassie pushed Reid toward the couch, and the second he complied in sitting, she climbed up onto his lap like it was where she belonged. My breath snagged at how perfectly she fit atop his thigh, and zero trace of alarm attempted to cool my blood.

The pink pig show she loved had started, and Cassie's attention immediately glued to the TV once more.

Reid turned his head and met my gaze over the back of the couch, one brow quirked along with his lips.

And that was that.

I sat beside him, keeping enough distance between us that I didn't appear needy but could still feel the heat of his body.

He appeared completely at ease with a little kid on his lap, and I reminded myself he had five nieces and nephews. I didn't know what to say—or as always in his presence— how to feel about the desire he brought to life inside me.

While his gesture with the gift I'd saved for later appeared friendly, the desire in his eyes suggested hope for more than a mere platonic relationship. Why the hell would he want to get involved with me when he had countless women paying for his skills in the bedroom? Not that I'd enjoyed *complete* satisfaction on our one evening together, but damn.

The thought of his hands on me again, the feel of his lips caressing my mouth, the taste of his languid tongue sliding over mine...

Raw heat swept through me, dampening my old cotton panties.

I dared a glance over at him.

A small smile lay on his face like a sprawling cat—content and eyes half-lidded as he returned my stare.

"She's beautiful just like her mom," he whispered.

"Shush!" Cassie barked without looking away from her show.

One of Reid's eyebrows quirked again. "Bossy," he mouthed.

"You have no idea," I whispered. "Christine likes to call her bossy-boo."

"Shush!" Cassie said again, glaring at me. "Peppa on!"

"Sorry, honey." I reached over and smoothed her hair back. Yeah, she was spoiled, but I enjoyed her little independent spirit that matched mine. I expected that didn't bode well for my future when she became a teenager, but I would enjoy every second until those days hit.

Reid nodded toward the kitchen, a question in his eyes.

I held up two fingers and mouthed, "Two minutes," knowing if we moved before Cassie became a cartoon zombie, she'd only demand we stay right where we were.

Hands on my knees, I waited, my thoughts flitting around so fast I couldn't complete one before another began. Safety and security were swept away by loneliness and yearning. My own stubbornness to keep men at arm's length dissolved at the potent connection radiating between me and Reid.

With expert ease, he slid from beneath Cassie and set her back against where he'd sat. She didn't spare him a glance as he tiptoed around the couch. He laid a hand on my shoulder and squeezed, sending a zap of lightning straight to my core.

I followed him from the room, my heart thumping like mad even though having him in our space felt...right.

Chapter 19

Reid

I leaned against the counter and held out a hand. Jessie had paused just inside the kitchen, arms banded around her waist, her gaze glued to my face. She wore no makeup, her face flushed, and hair escaped her sloppy bun. Too-large clothes draped over her curves same as last time I'd dropped by unannounced but didn't hide her unbound breasts and peaked nipples.

My teenage wet dreams come to life, Jessie made me want things no woman ever had—including Tara.

"Come here," I said, keeping my voice down so as not to disturb Cassie, but my lowered tone betrayed what the sight of Jessie did to my body.

She hesitated, one eyebrow raised, and I wiggled my fingers, impatient to feel her in my arms again.

Huffing, she took a few steps and slid her hand into mine.

I tugged, and with an oomph, she flattened against my chest. "I'm a mess," she stated quietly, staring at my pecs while I fought to keep from pressing my thickening dick against her belly.

"You're beautiful," I argued while tucking hair behind both her ears and lightly cradling her cheeks.

She lifted her gaze, searching my face. "This doesn't feel like mere friendliness. Why are you here, Reid?"

"You know why," I stated quietly, my patience over being just friends gone. She'd relented by allowing me into her apartment, a sure sign she'd begun to lower her walls. But I longed to take up actual space in her life.

"What man wants a woman with baggage?" she asked rather than spouting off excuses about trust and the need to focus on her daughter's life like I'd expected and hoped not to hear.

"You did *not* just call your beautiful little daughter a liability."

"No. It's just that—"

"If anything, she's an asset. She's a Jessie mini-me, so it's kind of like a two-for-one deal in my book."

Jessie's lips pursed, and she narrowed her stare into a *yeah right* look.

"Go out with me," I demanded what I'd been desperate for since walking out of that hotel room a few weeks earlier.

"I can't afford you."

"I'm a simple carpenter with callouses on my hands."

She cocked her head to the side. "What about Elite?"

"I set that part of my life aside after our date."

Her cheeks flushed again as I caressed over them with my thumbs, the pink spreading down her neck. So damn soft...I remembered how the rest of her skin had felt beneath my hands when she'd allowed me to oil her up and bring her release.

My dick twitched inside my jeans, desperate for a taste of what she had understandably denied me that night.

"Go out with me," I whispered again, desperation like a

raging hunger making me mad with need.

"It's not easy for me to find a sitter. I won't just leave Cassie with anyone."

I dared to hope over her lack of an outright no, ready to offer whatever she required to bend to the magnetism between us. "Then we'll take her with us."

Her mouth opened, but I put a finger over her lips. "No more excuses. Just say yes. We'll go to the ocean tomorrow. Collect seashells, swing on the playground swings, get ice cream, and take selfies."

"I don't do selfies."

I grinned over her grasping at straws to find an excuse to accept what had started between us. "Thank God, cuz I can't stand the damn things anyway."

She inhaled a deep breath before she bit down on her lower lip.

"What?" I asked, tugging the abused flesh from between her teeth. She stayed pressed against me but glanced away. "What?" I repeated while lowering my head to capture her focus.

Her worried gaze met mine. "While I've really enjoyed the past couple of weeks of getting to know you better as a friend, I'm not the type of woman who can haphazardly involve herself with someone. It's not just my heart at stake here." Jessie stepped back from me, and I let her go, my heart falling along with my hands from her sides. She crossed her arms over her chest, attention still riveted on my face as though trying to root out my secrets, my true intentions toward her and her daughter.

"I'm falling for you, Jessie." Her breath caught, but I plowed on, ready to lay it all on the line because I couldn't move on without *knowing*. "I love your honesty, your passion for being a mother, and your dedication to keeping that little stinker safe. You're sexy as hell and intriguing enough I swear I've slept all of twenty or so hours the last couple of weeks."

"I can't sleep either," she whispered.

The corner of my lip rose as the desire to lighten her haunted eyes rose to mind. "Been thinking about me while lying alone in your bed at night?"

I expected an eye roll or a light laugh.

She did neither.

"Your fingers. Your lips," she answered honestly, and her gaze honed in on my mouth as a shiver rippled through her. "Your tongue."

A curse dragged its way through my head as my dick bucked in my jeans.

Two strides and I grabbed her by the waist with one hand, the other on her neck, and kissed her like Armageddon blazed the earth around us. She fisted my shirt and held on tight as I ravaged her.

She *had* to feel what I did: full-on body tension yet an ease of rightness sliding into place inside my soul.

The sweetness of her tongue clenched my abs and eased pre-cum from my slit. Her exhale into my lungs gave me life. The unleashing of pent-up passion ripened to bursting with delicious satisfaction I could feel inside my bones even without the release of a climax. I gently bit and suckled my way down her neck, pulling a deeper moan from the chest I wanted to explore and slowly mark up if she'd let me.

"I won't sleep with you," she said as I ran my lips back upward to trace her ear with my tongue.

"I'll keep my dick to myself. Promise," I murmured before suckling on her lobe.

A shudder rippled down through her, but she leaned her head away, despite my need to taste more of her.

Not yet ready to give her up, I allowed her space but didn't let her past arm's length. "So...ocean and ice cream only." I wound my fingers in the excess cotton of her shirt at her hips to tighten my grip and keep her prisoner until she agreed. "Until you beg me otherwise."

She smacked my chest while biting back a smile. "Cocky jerk."

I kissed her again, taking my good old time turning her pliant beneath my lips while keeping my hands firmly fixed in her shirt. I didn't stop tasting her skin from the neck up until she sagged against me in complete surrender.

She had to feel my hard length pressed against her belly, but I held that part of me still, having promised to keep him out of the equation even though he wept to become acquainted with Jessie's warmth.

"I won't hurt Cassie," I vowed while losing myself in Jessie's whiskey eyes. "And I won't hurt you. I'm not like him."

"I know you're not." She heaved a sigh while glancing back at the living room. How was her checking in with her daughter a turn-on for me? Why did I find her instinctive need to shield her child so damn sexy? Jessie returned her attention to me, her gaze settled. Determined with a hint of stubbornness that I found too damn arousing. "Okay. We'll go with you tomorrow." She poked my right pec with a hard fingertip. "But *no sex*."

"No sex," I agreed and grinned, barely containing my desire to pump my fist in the air and shout out my excitement over conquering the first of Jessie's walls.

I walked out of their apartment a minute later, waiting to hear the two locks clicking into place. Glancing down at my raging hard-on, I told myself I could be patient for as long as she needed.

Chapter 20

Jessica

Cassie perched on Reid's shoulders, giggling like mad as he ran through the sand, chasing after seagulls and sending them into flight. Lightness filled me with all the warmth of the sun descending toward the horizon, and strangely, for the first time in months, no worry over the future ate at my stomach.

I laughed along with my daughter, uncaring that my heart had softened toward Reid. Unable to help myself, I fell harder for him with his every word, gaze, and action. From the long talks we'd shared to the Princess Sophia coloring book and crayons he'd gifted Cassie for using the big girl potty, he revealed his attentive nature. His agreement to keep sex out of the equation, while baffling, only endeared him to my heart.

We'd spent hours splashing along the edge of the ocean, and he hadn't tired of Cassie's demands to push her on the playground's swing again and again.

It had been my insistence to chase the birdies that finally got her out of the little kiddie area.

"How 'bout some ice cream, Munchkin?" Reid asked

my daughter, short of breath and patting Cassie's shin beside his neck as I caught up to them.

"Ice key! Ice key!" She kicked her feet, her bare heels thumping against his upper pecs.

"Cassie! No kick!" I admonished.

"Don't worry about it." Reid tightened his hold on her ankles to still her movements and smiled over at me. Happiness radiated between us, bringing butterflies alive in my stomach like they'd been doing on and off all day.

"Ice key!" Cassie insisted again, eyes the same color as mine flashing in the setting sun.

"Okay, Bossy-Boo." I trudged through the sand toward the steps up through the surge wall hiding the road from view, more than ready to sit and enjoy a strawberry frap.

Ice cream in hand, we settled at a picnic table beside the Creamery Shack. Cassie attacked her cup of vanilla with rainbow sprinkles, and I studied Reid as he stared at her, a soft smile fixed on his face.

"You'd think you never saw a little kid eat ice cream the way you're watching her," I said before fitting my straw between my lips for a slurp. Cold sweetness hit my tongue as Reid turned toward me.

"She's cute as a button."

I swallowed my mouthful of strawberry frap and smiled. "She is."

"Just like her momma."

I grimaced.

"What?" He laughed.

"I'd prefer something like hot or sexy."

"Neither word does you justice."

Warmth swept through my face, and I busied myself with my frap, every cell in my body wishing I hadn't set the no-dick rule into place. It had been so long, and I was so damn thirsty for Reid's flavor on my tongue and his gorgeous body on mine.

But I expected sex with him would be way more intimate than penetration and release. He would alter my reality. Ruin me for anyone. Definitely give me fantasy fodder for a lifetime.

All I had to do was ask, and he would show me the world, I had zero doubts.

But it couldn't possibly last, could it? And was I willing to take that chance?

"Lucky straw." Reid all but groaned the words, and I jerked my head up, cheeks burning like the rest of my body. "Sorry." He shrugged and ran his tongue around the tall vanilla and chocolate twisted soft serve while winking. "Couldn't help myself."

My gaze followed his tongue as he took another round, thoughts of his face between my thighs wetting my panties to the point I expected I might leave a smear on the seat beneath me.

Tearing my focus off Reid, I noticed rainbow-tinted ice cream dripping down Cassie's chin, two sprinkles stuck to one corner of her mouth. I grabbed a napkin to clean her up, my gaze flitting back to Reid again.

His dark eyes twinkled with a knowing look. The cocky prick knew exactly what I'd been imagining while watching him love on that cone. The same thing he'd been thinking while I'd sucked my straw. I made a humph sound and cleaned my daughter's chin.

"No way!" she shrieked, jerking away, hand covering the cup in front of her.

"I'm not taking your ice cream. Mommy just needs to wipe up this mess before you get it all down the front of your shirt."

"Ice key! Reid, ah ice key!"

The sexual tension left my shoulders as I smiled. "Yes, Reid bought you ice cream, but you didn't say thank you, did you?"

"Sank oo!" She grinned at Reid, and his returned smile melted whatever resolve I had.

♃

"Want to come in?" I asked as Reid pulled his truck into my apartment building's parking lot to drop us off

"No s-e-x," he spelled, not bothering to hide his smirk.

"I have half a bottle of wine in the fridge," I said rather than getting into details of what I might or might not want by prolonging our date. "It's cheap rosé but cold."

He put his truck into park. "Definitely."

We walked up to the front stoop, Cassie once more on Reid's shoulders. I punched in my code, not bothering to hide it from Reid, and opened the door to let him pass through. He had to duck to keep Cassie from bumping her head.

She giggled and pulled his hair to get him to straighten. "Up, goggie!"

"He's not your doggie," I said with a snicker.

"Reid mah goggie!"

"I'll be your doggie, munchkin." Reid patted her leg, and I stepped around them to lead the way up to the second floor. Once inside, I tossed my purse on the kitchen table and held out my arms.

"No way!" Cassie grabbed Reid's hair again.

Shaking my head, I pointed toward the living room. "See if she'll let you deposit her butt on the couch. I'll turn on Sophia."

"Phia! Phia!" Cassie chanted as we walked into the living room.

Lucky for Reid's hair follicles, my daughter let him put her down while I clicked on the TV. She flopped her head onto her blankie we'd left there earlier in the day, her gaze glued to the screen.

"I'll grab the wine," Reid said, tipping his head toward the kitchen.

Rather than waiting for him to return, I followed on his heels, every hair on my body wired as though on a coffee high.

"I'm actually going to be able to pay my car payment on time this month," I said, fighting to keep my sudden nervousness at bay while pulling two glasses from the cabinet and setting them on the counter.

Reid poured equal measures into both, emptying the bottle. "Way to go, Idaho."

I laughed and accepted the glass he held out to me. His fingers trailed over mine in the exchange. A shiver licked down my spine. "Cassie isn't old enough for Toy Story just yet."

He tipped his glass up, and swallowed, his Adam's apple bobbing and making my mouth water. "Being a goggie is hard work."

We both laughed quietly, and I sipped the inexpensive wine he hadn't grimaced over. We drank another swallow in silence, but I didn't mind the hovering stillness. Sexual tension had strung tight between us since he'd picked me and Cassie up, and I hadn't once shifted away in wariness from his intentional brushes against my body.

He'd teased me all damn day. Lingering hand on my lower back. Similar trailing of fingers over mine whenever we'd handed things to each other.

"What are you thinking?" Reid asked, his focus on my chest and the hard nipples I felt poking against my thin bra.

"Sex," I answered without thought.

"*No* sex, you mean." He lifted his gaze to my eyes, and the desire in his dark orbs made my knees go weak.

"More like the throw-me-to-the-floor-and-pin-me-down kind of sex." My voice escaped breathless with need, but the arousal he made me feel took me past the point of caring. One casual fuck and a few good orgasms to get me through the next couple of celibate months or years.

Reid groaned and lifted his wine. "There's a kid in the other room, or I would gladly make that dream come true."

"It's almost her bedtime."

We stared at each other, the quietness around us suddenly no longer as peaceful as it had been before my obvious invitation.

"You're serious?" He finally broke the silence.

"I'm not looking or hoping for a fairytale ending," I assured him even though thoughts of that exact thing would be a dream come true. "Just sex."

"What if I can't do that?"

I frowned. "You're a pro, Reid. Don't get all shy on me now that I'm finally giving in."

A flicker of something I couldn't discern glinted in his eyes, and he glanced away, putting his drink on the counter beside him.

"Mah," Cassie mumbled from the other room.

"I'm going to put her to bed, but you're welcome to stay," I said.

"I think I'm going to take off."

I didn't let my disappointment show on my face, but the surprise of being denied had to have shown through. Baffled

—and slightly hurt—I forced myself to accept his decision even if it did suck. "Okay."

"Harper's Construction is having a work party tomorrow. Would you and Cassie like to go with me?"

The sense of having done something wrong, of his suddenly being turned off and no longer interested in getting me into the sack, dissolved at his invite. He wanted us to meet his co-workers, his best friend, and Wren.

How could I not let hope soar through me even though the prospect of more than mere sex scared the shit out of me?

"We'd love that."

Chapter 21

Reid

I hadn't wanted to go to the work picnic by myself because I knew my friends would all be wrapped up in their lovers as usual, causing jealousy to streak through me. Wren busied herself at the food table, her gaze crossing the pavilion countless times to check in with Blake. Madeline labored alongside her to get things ready, and Colton leaned against Hudson, both not bothering to keep their lustful eyes off the woman who made up their triad.

A few other families had brought their kids, and for the first time since I'd been working for Harper's Construction, I had the pleasure of being involved in their antics because I hadn't arrived alone. Many children had brought bikes and tricycles to the park, and I helped Cassie keep her seat on a tricycle one of the younger girls had shared with her.

Jessie stood off to the side, taking pictures and calling out how proud she was of Cassie.

My heart felt near to bursting with contentment. Sure, I hadn't gotten to taste Jessie beyond her mouth the night before because I'd gotten butt hurt over her probably unintentional dig at me being a professional escort, but I'd gotten over it, and hope for so much more was as sweet as candy on my tongue.

Having the two of them with me felt right, gave me a sense of satisfaction I'd never experienced before—and craved more of.

Cassie had her fill of the little bike, grabbed her mom's hand, and dragged her toward the playground area to our right.

"Reid!" Blake called, and I angled toward him rather than following after the girls.

My best friend approached along with Colton, two cold longnecks in his hand. He held one out, and I took it gladly, tipping it back to cool my throat with the taste of hops. "You're smitten as fuck."

"Yep." I didn't bother arguing or letting my grin out.

"What did Micah have to say about your quitting Elite?" Colton asked. He'd gone to part-time for Blake, working on building a house-flipping business of his own, so I hadn't seen him a whole lot in the previous couple of weeks to fill him in on the saga of my life.

"He made me feel replaceable just like Jarod had said he would."

"He's a cold-hearted prick," Blake said without an ounce of meanness in his tone.

"Nah," I disagreed, going with Jarod's explanation he'd given me over the phone a couple of weeks earlier. "Micah's just a good businessman who keeps friendship out of the day job."

"So you're good?" Colton asked.

"Yep."

"And never been happier," Blake added.

I swallowed down another mouthful of pale ale and

nodded. Even without the sex, I'd never experienced a more satisfying relationship.

"Is she the one?"

I glanced over at Colton whose gaze had once more strayed to his curvy woman and her silver fox husband behind the food table. "Possibly," I answered. "How are things with your mommy and daddy?"

Colton muttered a curse at me, but he couldn't hide the color rising across his cheeks.

I chuckled and clinked my bottle against his. "I love riling you up."

"Fuck off," he whispered since kids scampered nearby.

Breathing deeply, I soaked in the warmth of the nearly too-hot sun and trailed my gaze after Jessie then Cassie. Mini-Me sat atop a slide, jabbering down at her mom who stood at the bottom, waiting for the little girl to giggle her way to the bottom. Jessie wiggled her fingers, her smile wide, the love in her eyes as she gazed at her daughter sending a pang through my chest.

I rubbed over my pecs, grinning like a fool.

"That little girl is an excellent start to the baseball team of kids you've always wanted."

Tearing my focus off my girls, I gave Blake my full attention. He'd known me almost my entire life and had met my sisters and most of their offspring. As my best friend, he'd listened to me lay out my dreams about finding the perfect house I could share with my soulmate and the numerous children I'd dreamed of having.

"She could be," I said after a few seconds of thinking about that. Falling for Cassie came as easily as it had with her mom. A two-for-one deal, a prospect that didn't turn me off in the least.

Cassie released her hold on the slide handles and

rushed downward, shrieking like a banshee. "Mah!" She giggled as Jessie swept her off the end up into her arms, lifting her toward the sky.

"Welcome to the club." Blake elbowed me, and I realized my face must have betrayed the exact emotions roiling inside my heart and mind.

How had those two girls entangled me in the creeping vines of ensnarement? How had they drawn me in and attached themselves so damn deep inside my soul?

I had no fucking clue—and I didn't care.

If pain lay in my future, I would gladly deal with it as long as I had the chance to taste heaven for just a little while longer.

Chapter 22

Jessica

"That boy has it bad for you," Wren told me, her focus on the group of men Reid stood with, one being the man she'd newly gotten engaged to.

I didn't bother disagreeing with her observance. Throughout our day at the park, I'd felt Reid's gaze on me.

"For Cassie too," Madeline tacked on from my other side.

We sat in lawn chairs beneath a maple tree beside the pavilion. Both women had accepted me into their little clique with welcoming arms. Even though I knew Wren had gotten a piece of Reid I'd yet to taste, no envy or jealousy over her threesome with the two best friends bothered me.

What Reid had done prior to meeting me didn't matter —including his sex work for Elite. There was nothing I could do about his past, same as mine lay behind me forever, so what was the point of getting upset over what used to be? At least he didn't have fear over lingering threats haunting his mind from time to time.

My daughter sat propped atop her doggie's shoulders

where Reid stood chatting with the other men. She no longer tugged on his hair, simply resting her cheek atop his head. Her eyes hadn't yet closed, but I could tell by her limp arms hanging at her sides she wasn't far from passing out cold.

It had been a second long day of play in the sunshine in a row, and I didn't doubt she would be out for the count and sleep through the night.

Arousal slid through me at the thought of going home and inviting Reid to stick around for a while. I was more than ready to end that no-sex rule. He'd chosen a second day of proving his sincere intentions before asking for more. I expected I would be the one to make the first move since he seemed hell-bent on showing me I could trust him being in our lives to gain access to my body.

"What kind of man is he?" I asked the two women since they'd known Reid a lot longer than I had.

"The family kind," Madeline answered first. "He wants a ton of kids, so if you're not up for having more or adopting, don't fall too hard."

She didn't tell me anything I didn't already know. Reid had been candid about his dreams for the future he'd given up on after his bitch ex had broken his heart.

"Jessie's already done," Wren told Madeline with a snicker. "Stick a fork in her. Am I right?" she asked me.

I smiled. "You're not wrong." Damn, it felt good to state the truth aloud. Oxygen rushed into my lungs as I expanded my chest, flooding my bloodstream with adrenaline.

Reid glanced my way and winked causing butterflies to erupt in my belly.

Madeline patted my arm. "Welcome to the family."

Family.

My eyes suddenly stung, and my smile wobbled. I

hadn't truly been a part of one ever, but I felt it deep in my soul in that moment. Warmth, contentment, flooded through me even as my throat tightened. I had longed to give Cassie the same as much as I strived to keep her safe. Had the gift of a night on the town actually brought my dreams to reality? And even more importantly, did I have the strength to trust Reid and allow a future with him to unfold?

One thing I knew for certain—I was more than ready to experience what I'd missed out on our first date. I kept my fingers crossed the stars aligned in my favor.

ℋ

I sat in the back of Reid's extended cab with Cassie so I could chat with her and keep her from falling asleep. If she napped on the way home, she wouldn't go down for me when we got there. The last thing I needed was for the stinker to get a second wind at 7:30 when I had other hopes for the night.

Reid snickered at me as I made Cassie sing with me and answer every question I could come up with about that pink pig she loved and the princess whose hand-me-down shirt she'd insisted on wearing to the picnic.

I asked about her favorite food, her new friend she'd made in the sandbox, and if she was excited to tell her friends in daycare about the weekend she'd had.

Finally, Reid turned into our apartment complex's parking lot, and I let out a groaned exhale of relief. He drove in the opposite direction of the entrance, pulling his truck into one of the visitor spots. An assumption on his part but one that let me know we were on the same page as to how our night would progress.

His gaze flicked to mine in the rearview mirror as he put the truck into park.

I smiled, heat unfurling in my belly as it had every time when our eyes met throughout the day. Add in the soft touches and brushes of his body against mine and I'd been primed and ready to go for hours.

"Goggie," Cassie murmured sleepily, lifting her arms out toward him.

"You can have your doggie in one minute," I told her, turning to unbuckle the straps keeping her in her car seat.

Reid hopped out first then opened the door beside me as I gathered Cassie into my arms. The second I climbed from the truck, she wiggled, reaching for him.

"Hey, Bossy-Boo," he murmured, snuggling her against his chest.

My eyes stung again, but I turned away to unhook her seat from Reid's truck. I lugged the contraption toward the front of our building where my car sat, Reid whispering against my daughter's hair the entire time.

Excitement for the rest of the night gave my footsteps extra bounce. Reid coming into our lives had infused energy in my bones, and I soaked in the sweet ache in my chest where my heart thumped with heavy beats.

Once I got Cassie's seat back into my car, we headed inside, the tense silence between him and I a live wire of crackling energy. At the rate we traversed the tightrope lessening in distance between us, he and I were sure to combust upon crashing into one another.

He was either going to have to swallow my cries or stuff my face in a pillow when I came because the euphoria would hit hard and long. Even if Reid ended up being mediocre rather than the pleasure-giving professional I expected, I would lie sated and thoroughly spent once we finished.

High expectations, but I'd gone long enough without dick that anything other than silicone or a vibrator would rock my world.

Hands shaking, I unlocked our apartment door and waited for him to walk deeper inside before locking us in for the next couple of hours at least.

Reid turned and looked at me, his arms full of clinging toddler, naked desire in his gaze as he took me in. A slow smirk curled his lips as he caught sight of my hardened nipples. He cocked an eyebrow, and heat flooded my face.

Attempting to regulate my breathing, I set down my bag on the kitchen table and moved in to take my kid from him. "Come on, baby," I cooed, and she sagged into me, nothing but sleepy, moldable muscle and bone.

Cassie snuggled into my breast, and I kissed her hair which smelled of ozone and sunshine. If Reid had dropped us off and run, I'd have bathed her for sure—but she would be fine until morning.

"Be back in a bit," I murmured, and he nodded.

I managed to brush Cassie's teeth and get her into a nightie, once more chatting the entire time to keep her eyelids from fluttering shut. She burrowed into her blankie without complaint, but I sat and read Goodnight Moon to the end.

Her mouth hung open until I finished.

"Be a good girl and sleep through the night for Mommy," I whispered before kissing her forehead.

Pulse once more thrumming, I flicked on her monitor and noise machine, then firmly shut her bedroom door behind me.

After a day outside in heat enough to make me sweat, I wasn't feeling the cleanest. Lower lip between my teeth, I traversed the short hallway and found Reid sitting on the couch, sprawled out and relaxed. He looked good in my personal space.

Hell, he looked mighty fine regardless of our long day.

"Did she go down for you alright?" he asked, patting his knee in invitation.

I hesitated from moving farther into the room. "Yeah. She loves her bed when she's this tired. It's one of the rare moments she doesn't holler 'no way' at me when I say it's time to do something."

"Come here." Reid motioned toward his lap again.

Pointing over my shoulder, I swallowed hard. "I-I was thinking we could shower first? I feel gross."

"We?"

I licked my lower lip. "Yeah."

"As in together."

Voice ripped away by nervous anticipation, I nodded and swallowed hard.

Reid hopped up and closed the distance between us with a few hurried steps. "Sex is a go," he asked for clarity.

"Yes," I whispered.

He leaned down and brushed his lips over my ear, causing a shiver to slide down my spine. "What if she wakes up?" His tongue flicked over my lobe, and I had to fight to find my thoughts and vocalize them.

"She's out cold and will be for hours, but I have a monitor in every room just in case. And she never gets out of her bed alone. Even in the morning, she'll call for me first."

Nosing down my throat, Reid let out a low, rumbled groan. "Lead the way, beautiful."

He took my hand, and I did as told, our footfalls hushed by the hallway's carpet. No sounds rose beyond the whirl of the noise machine behind Cassie's bedroom door.

I pulled two towels from beneath the vanity as Reid kicked off his shoes. By the time I turned, he'd tugged off his T-shirt too.

"Oh good lord," I gasped at the sight of his bare torso. A cramp of pure lust contracted my core as my gaze slid over prominent pecs, traveled down a bumpy road of abs, and stalled out on his luscious V disappearing into his jeans.

His fingers toyed with the button, and I swallowed hard. "You're drooling," he murmured.

I snorted. "How could I not?"

"You need to catch up with me."

Blinking, I lifted my focus to Reid's dark eyes, which twinkled with silliness and heat in equal measures.

My heart raced, and I held his gaze while kicking away my flip-flops. I lifted my tank top off overhead and pushed down the billowy linen pants. In nothing but damp panties and bra, I breathed deep, readying myself to strip naked even though he'd already seen and touched all of me.

"Stop," he murmured, moving closer to grasp my hand from unclasping my bra. "Let me fulfill my first fantasy."

Warm, calloused palms smoothed over my shoulders and to the middle of my back. Head tipped, I kept my focus on his eyes as he undid my bra and slowly slid it off my arms.

Reid's gaze flitted to my breasts. "Fuck." He gathered both in his hands, slowly thumbing my nubs until I panted.

My girls weren't the perkiest after breastfeeding, but he didn't seem the least bit disappointed by their sagging weight.

"The things I want to do to you, Jessie," he rasped quietly while pressing in even closer. Hands sliding up my neck to my face, he closed the distance and took my mouth in a hungry kiss that left my mind reeling and knees weak.

"Taste so good—so sweet," he murmured against my lips, hand fisting in my hair.

I allowed him to lead, angling my head with his tight grip so he could dive in deeper. Steal my breath. Empty my mind. I mapped out the hard, flinching muscles covering his torso, moaning over his perfection and how he ate at my mouth.

"Your body is insane," I replied once he ceased sucking on my tongue.

Pulling back a bit, he smirked, the twinkle in his eyes causing need to pulse through my core.

"Shut up," I muttered, going for his waistband and the button and zipper hiding what my entire body craved. "Want to taste you."

"Ah, fuck." He groaned as I sank to my knees and peered up at him, waiting for permission. "Do it. Take me out and suck my cock."

Heart thrumming, I focused on making Reid feel as good as he did for me.

Chapter 23

Reid

Lower lip between her teeth, Jessie popped my button and pulled down my zipper. A mess of blonde hair hung down her back, her pupils had blown with desire. She looked like a goddess hellbent on worshiping me.

I hissed as she tugged my jeans to my ankles. While I slid my feet free from the denim, she ran her palm along my hard length trapped behind my boxer briefs.

"You're so hot. Hard."

Pre-cum oozed from my slit, creating a dark spot on the tenting fabric. "For you," I rasped out, pressing into her light touch. Fuck, did I need friction.

Swallowing as though she truly drooled for a taste, Jessie grasped the waistband of my boxers and pulled them slowly toward the floor.

My dick caught on the edge but sprang free and bobbed in her face as she dragged them lower.

Quick breaths raised her flushed chest, and she wrapped her hand around my base as I kicked my underwear away. She whispered a desperate curse, causing my length to buck in her hold.

"You're killing me." I groaned, never having met a woman dead set on giving head when she knew I wanted to get my hands on her body.

She cupped my balls and took me into her hot mouth, tongue swirling over my glans in a wet, sensual lick.

"Jesus." I gritted my teeth and grabbed hold of her head to keep her from going to town and taking me over the edge before I was ready. Then again...giving her a mouthful if that was what she wanted ensured I'd last longer once I finally had her spread out beneath me.

She lathed and suckled along my length like my dick was her favorite flavor of lollipop, the wet popping noises every time she released my flesh tightening my balls. Finally—fucking finally—she took me fully into her mouth, sinking deep.

I hissed, fighting off the need to thrust until she gagged and tears rolled down her cheeks. "If you don't slow down, you're going to get more than you're probably wanting."

Jessie eased me from between her slick lips, her hand taking over as she peered up at me with eyes full of so much more than lust. "We have all night."

Fucking hell, the things my entire being longed for with that woman. "*All* night?"

"As long as you're gone before Cassie wakes."

I tightened my hold on Jessie's hair and tugged her toward my throbbing length.

She once more took me down without hesitation, and I groaned, tipping my head back, eyes closed.

While working for Micah, I hadn't had a single woman offer to suck my dick without being told to by their partner. Jessie's raw desire, her hunger, felt too. Goddamned. Good.

"Gonna come." I offered one last warning, tugging on her hair gently to pull her off me.

"Want it," she whispered with a moan and doubled down on her effort to make me fill her mouth.

"Fuck." I gave in, my groin tightening in readiness as my spine tingled and balls drew up. A pulse rippled through my taint, and I shot into her throat, grunting out curses.

She swallowed, attempted with the second spurt, and the third dribbled down her chin as she gasped for breath.

A tremor ripping through me, I eased her face away from my dick.

"Goddamn, Jessie." I wiped her chin and glistening lips with my thumb before yanking her upright.

Our mouths once more came together in a rush, and I lapped at the salty flavor of my cum on her tongue. Such a sweet, unselfish little lover...I wanted more.

I shoved down her panties and yanked her up into my arms.

"Yes," she hissed, her legs wrapping around my waist. The wet heat of her pussy settled on the root of my cock, which sagged enough to point downward, but I ground against her while eating at her mouth.

Fuck the shower and her feeling gross.

Turning, I pressed her back against the used towel hanging off a hook on the back of the bathroom door and palmed her ass cheeks.

"Let go," I told her, and she complied, unwrapping her body from mine so I could heft her higher and sink to my knees.

"Oh shit," she breathed as she shifted her legs onto my shoulders, allowing me to drop fully, face in line with her pussy.

Breathing deep, I nosed up through her lower lips, her

arousal slick and musky. My mouth watered, and at the first swipe of my tongue up through her core, she grabbed hold of my hair.

Eyes wide and cheeks flushed, she stared down at me, her mouth parted. I licked along her lower lips like I had my ice cream, and she let out a whimper.

"Please, Reid."

"Please what?" I kissed her hard, little nub.

"I need to come."

"Can you keep quiet?" I asked and licked up through her core again, coating my tongue with her tangy cream.

"Mmm," she murmured and nodded.

"Hold on, sweetheart. I'm about to blow your mind."

Her fingers tangled tighter in my hair as I lifted her hips even higher to access every inch of her.

Nose burying in her pussy, I ran my tongue across her puckered rosebud beneath, and she squirmed in my hold. She'd said yes to sex, and I was going to take whatever she allowed. I would lay claim to every hole in her body—even if she didn't realize I'd be making them mine.

"Please, Reid," she begged again, trying to angle her hips backward so my mouth would land on her clit.

"I'll get there, impatient girl. Let me have this second fantasy."

She relented, and I explored with my lips, tongue, and teeth. Had she been spread out on a bed, my fingers would have gotten involved, but I wasn't about to pause and move. I wanted her climaxing on my tongue.

Shoving said bit of flesh into her tight sheath, I curled the tip and felt over her silken walls, swallowing down every hint of her slick arousal I could gather.

"G-God." Jessie tipped her head back and pressed her chest toward me. "I'm going to come," she whispered.

"Give it to me," I murmured and sucked her clit between my lips.

She whined. Shuddered. And came with a sharp, short cry before swallowing it down and groaning through clenched teeth. Her pussy contracted around my thrusting tongue, but like a good girl, she kept her noises to a minimum until she melted against the door, her grasp on my hair lessening.

One down.

Many, many more to go.

I set Jessie onto her feet, keeping hold of her since she seemed a little unsteady, her glazed-over eyes a sweet shot to my ego. Rubbing my palm over my mouth rid my lips of the remnants of her climax. "You good?" I asked before releasing her fully with my other hand.

"*You're* good," she breathed and shivered.

Chuckling, I pressed my lips to hers for a quick, chaste kiss. "Gonna get the shower going, then map out your body for future reference."

"Mmm, 'kay."

I left her there, moving for the tub. A crate of bath toys sat in the back, so I pulled it out and set it on the floor before starting the water. Heat quickly took over the cold, and I turned the knob, sending the water up into the showerhead.

Jessie crossed the small space and stepped in while I held the curtain back for her.

I followed her in, enclosing us behind the plastic sheet that still smelled new.

Shifting her toward me, I once more laid claim to her mouth as water beat down on her back. Slow and gentle, I made love to her lips and tongue, learning the taste of her, committing her to memory in the event she wouldn't let me have her after that night.

Pushing aside depressing thoughts that I wouldn't be offered the gift of loving on her a second time, I set to touch every inch I could with soapy hands, worshiping her body and finding those little spots that made her sigh or shut her eyes in bliss.

She loved my tongue on her lower back and my hands rubbing up the insides of her thighs. Gentle nibbles on her shoulders earned me a sweet tremor. Licking over the shell of her ear leaked a whimper from her lips. Sucking on her nipples covered the rest of her in goosebumps, and my fingertips slick with soap over her puckered hole spilled curses from her lips.

"My turn," she insisted, her tone once more breathless with want.

Her hands ran over me, feeling up the muscles over my entire torso and thighs, easily and quickly swelled my dick for round two. When she took my thickening length in hand to stroke, I grabbed hold of her wrist.

She lifted her gaze to my face, and I swore on all things holy the woman felt the same draw and emotional attachment I did for her. I wanted to make her mine. Slide deep inside her soul and never leave.

But not in the shower.

I turned to rinse and shut off the water.

Without a word, we dried with almost threadbare towels, and I followed on her heels across the hall into her bedroom where she moved to her bureau to turn on that room's monitor. A soft whirring noise rose, the same as it had from the one atop the bathroom counter.

I fished my wallet from my jeans that I'd carried in from the bathroom. Two condoms were tucked inside, and I pulled them free, tossing them onto the bed before setting my jeans aside. Dropping the towel I'd tucked around my waist, I nodded toward Jessie's covering. "Get naked—let me see what I'm about to flush with arousal."

Smirking, she unwound the towel from around her breasts, and let it fall to the floor. A pink hue already tinted her skin, but from the hot shower or my loving on her body, I didn't know.

It didn't matter, either, because I was just getting started, and there were plenty more shades of red to go.

Chapter 24

Jessica

Reid pulled me up into his arms, then climbed onto the bed, laying me out beneath him. Planked, he stayed off my upper torso, the heat of his groin and hairy thighs a welcome weight along my lower body.

I ran my hands up his arms to his shoulders, loving the smooth skin and rippling show of strength in his muscles. The man was built like an absolute god and deserved to be on smutty book covers.

A few seconds passed as we stared at one another, a silent exchange of agonizing hesitation to prolong the excitement shimmering almost tangibly between us. Nothing existed at that moment but the need and desire to come together. Physically joining in intense intimacy that could very easily end up breaking either of our hearts.

"You're sure?" he whispered with zero hint of a negative concerning his own thoughts on what we were about to do.

"I want you." Three simple words were all it took for him to back off and grab a condom.

Heat rushed through me as I watched him roll the

rubber down over his impressive girth. I'd gagged a few times over his length in my mouth, and a slight ache still rested in my jaw from having stretched to wrap my lips around him fully.

But he'd been delicious on my tongue, and the sound he'd made while coming undone from my touch? Chef's kiss of spine-tingling perfection.

Once sheathed, he crouched down to kiss the inside of my thigh. He bit lightly on the other, and I splayed both open, granting him full access. Lifting my ass in his palms, he licked once more from my ass to my clit, rumbling in appreciation of my taste.

Another slow lick, and he stalled out at my pussy, tonguing in and around my lower lips, smearing my arousal and saliva over every inch. "So wet." He lathed at me again. "You're gonna feel so good wrapped around my dick. Fuck, do you turn me on, woman."

Back on his hands and knees, he moved upward, kissing my bare pubis I'd once more shaved. My belly button. The faint trace of stretch marks from my pregnancy. He stayed put over my silvery skin, tonguing along the lines and gently pressing his lips to them.

Tears stung my eyes, and I ran my fingers through his thick hair.

"You're so beautiful," he murmured.

I swallowed hard, my heels finding his ass as he meandered slowly up the rest of my body, pausing to love on my breasts and aching nipples too.

"Reid," I breathed out a desperate plea for him to hurry the fuck up even though I adored how he worshiped me.

Dragging his tongue up my neck, he finally found my lips to stroke inside.

His mouth...every bit of it should have been illegal.

Stamped with a warning of turning women into puddles of lustful need no rational mind could possibly resist.

A shift of our bodies brought the head of his dick where I needed it, and I tugged with my heels, whimpering over his lips.

He slid his tongue into my mouth—and sank his length into my body with one slow, torturous glide. Stretched beyond what I'd ever felt, I moaned, angling my hips to take him even deeper.

Reid lowered to his elbows and flexed his ass, giving me what I wanted.

I gasped as he pushed against my cervix, but his resulting groan sprang more arousal to life inside me.

"Fuck, Jessie." Reid pressed his forehead to mine, his hot breath ghosting over my parted lips. "You're so slick and hot. Jesus Christ." He groaned and lifted his head, dragging out along my inner walls.

Gazes locked, we moved in slow motion, the wetness of my core making for one sloppy, noisy mess that only made me hotter.

I ran my fingernails along the muscles lining his spine, curling upward with my hips as he sank deep inside me, another groan rumbling through his chest.

No stimulation rubbed over my clit, but the insides of my thighs and belly began to tingle with the promise of another climax.

"Oh God," I whispered, starting to shake.

"Gonna come on my cock already, sweetheart?"

"Mmm." I bit my lip.

"Keep your eyes on me," Reid said, continuing his slow rock in and out of my body. "I want to see you let go and come apart."

"H-harder—please."

"Nuh uh. Give it to me like this."

"Can't," I gasped, never having climaxed on an unhurried dick without outside stimulation on my clit.

Reid brushed his lips over mine. "I think you can. Your pussy is the sweetest place on earth. Listen to how wet you are for me."

Heat rushed over my skin, and I moaned at the lewd noises filling my ears.

"Feel how hard you make me, Jess." He pushed in deep, rolling his hips in a sensual grind that moved his pelvic bone over my throbbing clit.

"Oh god."

"Gonna come for me?"

"Yes—fuck, yes." A swell rose inside of me and crashed, shattering deep inside, clamping my core around his dick.

Reid cursed—and stopped moving completely.

My body undulated through its climax, pulsing around his girth, attempting to pull him deeper, to milk and wreck him like he did to me. Eyes hazing over in my bliss, I lost sight of him, my spine arching.

"So goddamn beautiful."

"Fuck—Reid, fuck me. Please," I sobbed as my climax ebbed, writhing beneath him because I was far from done.

He leaned down and bit my earlobe, his dick bucking inside me—but not releasing. "I want another one."

"Then move," I gasped out, digging my fingernails into his back. "For the love of God—"

He thrust, stabbing fully inside me.

My entire body jolted from his force, and I bit my lip to keep from crying out at the painful pleasure rippling through me.

"So. Fucking. Mine." Reid swore the words as though a vow before every saint imaginable with each thrust. "Jessie

—" He finally lost control, shoving into me with deep thrusts, dominating with unleashed power.

My lips bruised beneath his, the weight of his body pressing into me.

That saying about being fucked into the mattress? I finally understood its meaning. I was breathless. Powerless. Completely at the mercy of the mass of muscle atop me. His ass clenched beneath my heels, driving him into me with long, harsh strokes that made me desperate for more.

"Fucking hell." He growled and planked, peering down between us to see where he impaled me over and over. My arousal smeared over his entire groin, had wet the dark curls at the base of his dick, and dribbled over his tight balls. "Play with your little nub—want to feel you come again all over my cock."

My hand snaked between us without a conscious thought in my head.

"Mmm," I moaned as tingles raced through my body on a collision course with my pussy.

"Yeah—give it to me." He grunted and thrust.

I swallowed my shriek while bowing upward beneath him, my nipples tight and core clamping down around him.

"Fuck yeah." He once more held still while I shattered into a million pieces.

"Goddamn you!" I cursed and gulped, slapping at his shoulder. "Move! Please."

"Mmm." The fucker continued to enjoy being buried to the hilt while I pulsed and shuddered beneath him.

"Fuck," I cursed, gasping and shivering on a last tremor. "You...you *bastard!*"

He chuckled and pulled out. One hand on my hip flipped me onto my belly before I knew what he planned, further spinning my head.

"Oomph!" I released an exhale, and he yanked me up onto my knees. "Oh God," I moaned, my back arching as gentle fingers stroked over my lower, swollen lips and upward to circle my puckered hole.

"Anyone ever take you here?" Reid's voice was nothing but rumbled need, and heat once more flushed through me.

"J-just fingers." I shuddered as he pressed lightly, slipping in to the first knuckle without difficulty. "Oh fuck," I groaned, my back arching even deeper in invitation.

"One day, sweetheart." Reid withdrew his thumb and pressed his lips to the base of my spine. "Promise. Now hold on. This isn't going to be slow or gentle."

He grasped my hips and slammed into my pussy.

I cried out into the pillow, doing exactly as he'd said— grasping at the damn thing, giving it my curses and harsh moans.

"Goddamn." Reid slapped my ass cheek, and my backside lifted, seeking more. "Fuck yeah." His palm swatted the other. "So fucking sexy."

Palming my cheeks, he spread them wide, hammering into me with unrelenting force.

"You're taking me so well—such a good fucking girl, Jessie. Fuck, I'm gonna come."

I lifted onto my hands, pushing back toward his every stroke. "Yes," I cried, the wet flesh smacking together an erotic sound I'd never thought sexy before.

"Fuck!" Reid growled the word, his dick jerking harshly inside me. Deep groans rolled from him with every stuttered thrust of his hips.

My arms went limp, and I let him hold me up by my hips as he emptied in the condom. Eyelids fluttering closed, I wished his cum painted my insides. Mixed with mine and stayed in me long after he left.

Chapter 25

Reid

Jessie collapsed onto the bed beneath me, and I pulled out, sucking wind while planting another kiss against the base of her spine. Twin red handprints stood out in stark contrast to her white ass cheeks, and I grinned, running my tongue over them.

She made a noise of complaint but didn't move until I'd finished tasting her heated flesh.

Heaving a heavy sigh, I sat back on my haunches and rid myself of the full condom. A quick tie and I tossed it aside, telling myself I would pick it up later and find a trash can. I wished I'd been able to fill Jessie with my cum instead, plugging up my seed in her pussy with my slowly softening dick.

Maybe make a baby.

One day, I promised myself while kissing back up her spine, because yeah. We clicked in every way, fit together perfectly, and after having spent only two solid days with her and Cassie, I knew without a doubt that I wanted in on that shit forever and ever.

Nose in her still-damp hair, I rooted around, breathing in the scent of strawberries from her shampoo.

"Okay?" I asked, needing to check in since I hadn't taken it easy on her.

"That was incredible," she muttered into the pillow she once more hugged to her face.

Chuckling and my chest swelling with pride, I kissed her shoulder and rolled onto my back, one hand resting on her thigh. My heartbeat still thrummed, and I'd worked up one hell of a sweat. I hoped Jessie had another set of sheets somewhere.

The whirl of a soft motor reached through the monitor, assuring me we hadn't woken Cassie up. We hadn't exactly been quiet.

I turned my head at the same time Jessie did, and our gazes met and held. Same as right before I'd sunk into her warmth, we shared a silent moment. One full of hope and expectation. Connection and a sense of rightness that had only solidified in my heart and mind after the intimacy of what we had just shared.

Reaching out, I tucked strands of hair behind her ear.

Jessie shifted onto her side and curled up slightly, hand tucked beneath her cheek.

Fuck, I could drown in her whiskey eyes. Rolling in a similar fashion, I faced her, intent on doing just that.

The contentment and satisfaction on her face swept an even more intense sense of desire for more I'd already been feeling through my chest. Unable to keep my hands to myself any longer, I reached out to smooth back her hair, my thumb caressing lightly over her cheek.

A phone rang, infringing on the sweet moment.

"Shit." She snorted an exhale and sat up.

"Ignore it," I said, my hand falling to the warmth of the pillow she'd left behind.

"Can't." She moved for the edge of her bed with more energy than I'd have thought possible, considering how she'd collapsed beneath me. "No one ever calls me this time of night."

"Then it's probably spam," I said, rolling to my back and tucking my hands behind my head.

Her reddened ass jiggled as she hurried to open the bedroom door.

She ignored my suggestion, and I listened to her quick, pattering footfalls down the hallway.

"Hello?" Her voice carried from the kitchen, and anyone with half a brain would know what she'd been up to a few seconds earlier in the dimmed lights of her bedroom. "What?" she whisper-shrieked, erasing my grin.

I sat upright, my brow furrowing as a flicker of adrenaline coursed through me.

The TV clicked on.

"...considered armed and dangerous. If you have any information on his whereabouts, please call the number on the screen below."

Fuck. I grabbed both our towels and hurried out to the living room, wrapping one around my waist as I went.

Face pale and palm against her mouth, Jessie stared at the TV, the cell phone slipping from her grasp to tumble to the floor. "Oh, shit."

I stepped closer, noting her hitched shoulders and the tremors rippling through her. Opening the second towel, I moved in against her back to wrap her up.

A gasp ripped from her lips at my touch, and she spun. As our eyes met and recognition lit, she went limp and fell against me, giving me all her weight, which I easily held.

I glanced up at the screen in front of me. "Devon?" I asked through gritted teeth while taking in the black-and-white mug shot on the screen and tucking the towel around Jessie.

She nodded against my chest, a choked sob escaping past the hand she held to her mouth.

"Shh." I smoothed back her hair and kissed her forehead. "He doesn't know where you live. You're safe." At least, I hoped that was the case. She'd told me he sent monthly letters addressed to her at work and that she'd changed her last name prior to moving to her current residence.

"B-But what if he finds us?" she whispered, her voice small, sounding near broken.

I hugged her tighter, wrapping her up in my arms. "I'm staying the night," I said, not leaving any room for argument. The woman wouldn't be able to pry me from her personal space unless she called the cops to rid herself of my presence.

"But Cassie—"

"I'll leave in the morning before she wakes up."

"But—"

"There are no buts about it, Jessie," I stated firmly, my mind made up about my responsibility toward her and Cassie.

Devon didn't have the right to touch either of them as far as I was concerned, and I would do anything in my power to make sure she never had to lay eyes on the bastard ever again. "I'm not leaving you alone here tonight with that asshole on the loose."

She sniffed and shuddered but thankfully didn't argue with me.

"I'm going to double-check that the windows and door are locked up, okay?"

She nodded, putting a little space between us, still sniffling.

"You're going to go peek in at Cassie, then get dressed in some comfy clothes before crawling back into bed."

Biting on the inside of her lip, she peered up at me, her hands grasping at the towel slung around my waist. "I-I need to be close to her."

I'd been thinking the same exact thing. Nodding, I rubbed her arms, hating how cool she felt to the touch. "Do you have any sleeping bags?"

"No."

"Grab the extra blankets off your bed, and I'll get those two," I said, nodding toward the chair in the corner. "We'll camp out on Cassie's floor."

Relief flitted over her face. "Thank you, Reid."

I kissed her forehead again. "I'll keep you safe."

Nodding, she left my arms, clutched the towel close, and hurried back the hallway.

Flicking off the TV, I remembered the cell phone Jessie had dropped. I picked it up off the floor.

"Hello?" I said, holding it to my ear to see if whoever had called hadn't hung up.

"Reid?"

"Christine," I greeted, not surprised to hear her on the other end of the line.

"You're staying?"

"Yes."

"Good. And tell her not to worry about coming in tomorrow. I'll talk to my dad and make sure she's covered financially."

I'd already planned on doing the same except for talking to Mr. Gemberling. "I'll let her know."

I got off the phone a few seconds later, assured myself that Jessie's apartment was locked up tight, and made my way back to the bedrooms.

Cassie's door sat halfway open, and Jessie quietly spread out her comforter on the floor beside the toddler bed. She'd put on leggings and a long T-shirt like I'd told her to do.

Easing into the room, I kept as quiet as possible and handed over the blankets I'd brought from the living room. I pointed at my towel, then the hallway.

She nodded, seeming a little more settled but definitely less shaky.

I tugged on my boxer briefs and T-shirt after a quick pitstop in the bathroom.

Jessie lay curled on her side facing Cassie's bed when I returned.

Moving up behind Jessie, I pulled her backside against me and wrapped my arm around her waist. Her hair tickled my nose, and I leaned closer to kiss the top of her head.

"Try to get some sleep," I whispered. "I'm not going anywhere and will watch over you both."

It was some time after Jessie finally relaxed in my arms that my words returned to my mind. I wouldn't just keep her physically safe...I had every intention of shielding her heart and emotions free from harm too. Whether Jessie would like it or not, I'd found a new meaning to the phrase third wheel, and I planned on keeping that title for a long damn time.

Chapter 26

Jessica

Unbelievably, I slept like a baby—as did Cassie. I woke with the first beam of sunshine peeking through her heavy curtains. Stretching made me aware of the male body pressed against my back emitting luxurious heat. Far from a morning person, I'd never enjoyed the feel of morning wood against my ass before. The hard length of Reid though lit a fire in the soreness between my legs and set my heart to racing, regardless of how our night together had abruptly ended.

Our time together had blown away my expectations. My comfort level with him far outweighed what I'd experienced before with a man during sex. There hadn't been a single moment of discomfort, even when he'd lingered at my belly to kiss my stretch marks...as though he'd been appreciative of every one of them. Like he enjoyed seeing them because they reminded him of my daughter who had fallen head over heels in love with him.

Doing the same as Cassie had with Reid would be wicked easy. A simple step, an admission of getting caught up in something that seemed too good to be true.

But I knew better.

As quietly as possible, I slid forward and glanced over my shoulder to find Reid wide awake, his dark eyes on my face. Tingles slid through me like they always did whenever his gaze latched onto mine. However, we didn't have time to let the moment linger or make it into something more.

"You need to go before Cassie wakes up," I whispered.

Lips pursing in a thin line, he nodded and rolled off of our makeshift bed on the hard floor.

We tiptoed from the room, and I shut Cassie's door behind us. He hit the bathroom while I retrieved his jeans from the bedroom. Too much emotion, too many thoughts stumbled around in my mind like a bunch of toddlers, and I wanted nothing more than to go back to sleep to escape reality.

Fear warred with longing. Antsy jitters suggested retreat while the need for physical comfort demanded I wrap myself up in Reid's presence again.

Real life, the day ahead, decided for me.

I met Reid in the living room where he pulled on the rest of his clothes and put on his shoes. Once finished, he straightened and moved into my space, his hands clasping my face and calming my racing mind for the briefest of moments.

Giving in to my weaknesses pushed me to sink into him, to bury my face against his chest and breathe him deep into my lungs, but I refused, staying strong as I'd had to be for years on end.

Mondays meant reality whether I wanted it or not, and my stubbornness dictated I stand on my own two feet in the light of day.

"Christine said to stay home today and not worry about your paycheck," he said. "I talked to her last night."

Wetness filled my eyes, and I nodded, making a plan to call her as soon as Reid left.

The knowledge he needed to walk out the door and leave me and Cassie alone didn't sit right no matter how much I told myself I would be fine on my own and that he had to go to work.

"You going to be okay?" he asked, searching my eyes.

I nodded firmly but wasn't so sure.

"If you need me, please call. I'll get here as fast as I can."

Not trusting my voice, I nodded again.

He leaned down to swipe his lips across mine, lingering briefly. "I'll come back tonight if you want me to."

A pent-up exhale I hadn't known I needed to release deflated me. "I'd like that," I admitted with a whisper, tears continuing to clog my throat. "But only after Cassie is in bed."

His eyes dimmed at my statement, but he nodded. "Lock up behind me and don't let anyone in but me," he said, turning to leave.

I did as told and leaned against the closed door. Although I'd slept the night through, my head ached along with the inside of my thighs. I'd had fantasies of luxuriating in the sting of being put to bed completely sated someday by Reid Sullivan, but what had gone down afterward squashed all the warm fuzzies and the satiated bliss I'd dreamed about.

But what was done was done. I couldn't change the past or what Devon had managed to do. Safety came first, but as to what I could do, I wasn't sure. An escaped convict, he would never obey a restraining order even if I managed to get one.

Given the chance, he would find me and make me pay for helping to put him away exactly as he promised on a monthly basis with those damn letters. Coldness swept through me, settling into my bones. Desire for Reid's steadying presence rose to a choking level inside my chest.

Too good to be true rang in my head, same as when Devon had first started coming around, treating me like a precious princess he would cherish forever and ever. Something bad was bound to happen, so being on guard both physically and with my emotions was a necessity.

With a glance at the clock, I headed back to the living room for my cell.

"Hey, Jessie. How are you?" Christine asked upon answering.

"Scared shitless." I curled up on the couch and hugged my knees, my eyes closed.

"I can imagine. Sorry I called so late, but I figured you'd want to know."

Devon had escaped prison. Could be anywhere...

My eyelids shot back open, my gaze darting from the drawn curtains of my living room to the kitchen and front door. Stomach clenched and adrenaline rushing through my system, I fought to find my voice beneath my thickening throat. "I appreciate your call—and your assurance that I don't need to worry about work, but—"

"It's okay," Christine said as my tears fell. "I'll talk to my father once he shows up at the office and get you some extra personal time. He knows about the letters and would probably want you to stay home until Devon is found anyway."

More wetness coated my cheeks, and I struggled to whisper my thanks.

"I'll keep my fingers crossed they get that bastard soon. You stay inside and don't let anyone in."

"I-I won't," I somehow managed.

"Now get some coffee in you and go snuggle with your little stinker."

I smiled through my tears and nodded. "M'kay."

A half-hour later, Cassie called for me. My stomach churning and aching, I set aside the coffee I'd attempted to drink to go get her out of bed.

She sat up, bleary-eyed, her blonde hair a rat's nest. "Goggie?"

I laughed lightly, although her immediate request for Reid sent a pang through my chest. "It's just you and me today."

"Ah goggie!" She pouted so damn adorably that my heart squeezed.

"I know, baby." Part of me wished to tack on a *me too* as I lifted my daughter into my arms and covered her face with smooches, but with the news of Devon, memories about our years together had begun resurfacing in the earlier stillness while I sat alone in the living room.

I remembered his cursing me out, the way he'd belittled me, how the drugs had altered his mood more often than not. A smarter Jessie would have left him years prior to his incarceration. The idea of being tangled up in that relationship again—*any* relationship—made acid churn inside my belly.

I'd felt safe with Reid, and he'd never given me a reason to not trust him, but the emotional power he could hold over me if given the chance...

Swallowing against rising bile, I took Cassie into the kitchen and forced my attention onto filling her stomach and bathing her. While focused on my mundane tasks, I managed to keep my thoughts on the entire situation from taking over my body's responses.

With the TV running cartoons in the background, I

straightened up the immediate vicinity, refusing to leave Cassie's side.

Once she finished eating her cereal, I filled the tub and let her splash around without a care in the world while I sat on the laminate flooring, knees drawn up, my arms wrapped around them.

She giggled and played, jabbering all sorts of nonsense while I stayed silent—contemplative when I'd have preferred silence between my ears.

Falling for Reid was becoming too damn easy. So would letting him fully into our lives. But the wounds of my past demanded I protect both of us regardless of how my heart felt.

Chapter 27

Reid

I probably drove Jessie nuts with all of my checking-in text messages to her throughout the day, but I couldn't get her and Cassie off my mind. Imagining Jessie's fear for both herself and her daughter angered me to the point where I threw a few tools in frustration. God, did I want to punch something. Add in the fact that my craving for Jessie hadn't nearly been satisfied with our one night in her bed, and I was two exhales short of going on a rampage.

Thank fuck Blake and Wren had left for Cancun earlier that morning, so no boss looked over my shoulder to give me shit for my attitude. Colton had taken time off from his house-flipping business to join the crew working on the high school, so he decided to be Blake for the day.

He ordered me to take a break and call my woman, since hearing her voice would soothe me better than any text.

"Hi," Jessie whispered, the whirring sound of Cassie's noise machine obvious in the background and letting me know her daughter napped.

"How are you holding up?" I asked, and she must have

exited Cassie's room to chat since the soothing noise her daughter slept to faded, eventually shutting off completely.

"I'm alright." Jessie exhaled loudly in my ear and let out a tiny groan.

I expected she'd either sank onto the couch or her bed. "What have you two been up to?"

"Playing dress up in my clothes, coloring, making macaroni art. Anything to pass the time indoors since I'm not about to step outside."

"Good—please don't."

"I can't live like this forever though, Reid." Jessie's voice shook, and I longed to wrap her up in my arms. "The fear... it's too much. My stomach hurts. My head is pounding. I know the cops are looking for him, but they should stake out here because I have this feeling he's going to find me. He's always been a driven prick and won't stop until he gets his way. Pretty sure the past ten months' worth of letters are more than a hint of his first bit of business now that he's free."

"I'll do my own stakeout then," I promised. "And I won't stop until he's behind bars again."

"I..." She trailed off, and I waited for her to find her voice. "I'm sorry for being such a burden," she finally mumbled.

"The last thing you are is a burden, Jessie. You and Cassie have given me more happiness in the previous couple of days than I remember ever having felt before. It's like you slammed into me like a tornado, turned me around —fucking spun my emotions up to the bursting point—and yet I've never felt so peaceful."

She snorted what sounded like a sarcastic laugh. "Yeah, okay. Give Mini-Me some time. She'll send you running for the hills if I allow you the chance to get too close."

Fear laced her every word even though it sounded like she'd attempted to be flippant. I'd never had a child of my own, but I'd seen the instinctive need to protect in all three of my sisters. I understood, even though I hadn't personally experienced where Jessie's mind had to be.

"I'm serious," I insisted. "I told you that I won't hurt her —or you. Now isn't the best time, but damnit to hell, Jessie, I want to be a part of your lives, and leaving you this morning knowing you're shut up in the dark tore me up inside. I can't fucking stand it." I wanted to press my lips to her forehead, murmur assurances until she believed me, but distance meant I only had words to offer her. "Please give me a chance. Please."

"I-I told you I can't—"

"I'd do anything to be Cassie's and your third wheel," I rushed to say, desperation raising my voice and tripping my pulse. "*Anything*. Whatever you need, whatever you say, I'll do it."

Jessie didn't speak long enough that I checked my cell to make sure she hadn't hung up on me.

"Unfiltered, please," I begged, not wanting her to over-think what she wanted or didn't want to say. I needed a straight answer, but no matter her decision, I wouldn't leave her alone with Devon still on the loose. "Don't hold back your thoughts now."

"I'm falling for you, Reid." I could hear the wobbly smile in her voice, and a rush of elation eased the tension in my shoulders. "But I'm scared half to death of taking another chance. Of trusting a man with Cassie's heart, never mind mine."

"You *do* trust me, otherwise you never would have allowed me to spend the night."

She didn't reply.

"You're already offering me a chance, and you didn't even realize it." Fuck, I wanted to kiss her. "I'm heading to your place later this afternoon, but I'll wait outside until Cassie is in bed. We can talk more after, alright?"

"Yeah." The whispered answer didn't sound ecstatic, but at least it wasn't resigned like I'd forced her into giving me something she wasn't interested in.

Colton eyed me as I ambled back his way where he was helping a few guys frame out a stairwell. "Everything okay?"

Lips tight, I nodded.

"What do you know about this Devon asshole?" he asked.

I'd told Colton a little about Jessie's past but hadn't over-shared since her history wasn't mine to fill others' ears with. I'd kept the details to a minimum, letting Colton know Devon hadn't exactly been kind to Jessie.

"Anything your uncle can look into? Help with?" Colton suggested.

My uncle was the Chief of Police and was probably already well aware of the situation concerning Jessie's ex. I'd listened to every bit of news possible since leaving her apartment earlier that morning, pissed the police had yet to find the asshole but pleased they still had a massive search going on.

Devon had been called armed and dangerous, which meant he'd either escaped with a weapon in hand or they somehow knew he'd gotten access to firepower of some sort.

Either way, my stomach remained knotted, and I only managed to choke down half of the sub Colton had gotten us for lunch.

"The police are actively looking for him," I told my friend, "so I'm not sure what more Uncle could do." I shrugged, eyeing Blake's employees working a few feet from us.

"Does he know about Jessie?"

"You mean what she is to me?"

"Yeah."

I shook my head. "I haven't even told my parents yet—it's too new."

"*New* but real and potentially long-term, right?"

"Damn right, it is." I rubbed the back of my neck, taking stock of the soreness from a sleepless night on the floor and the rising tension making it ten times worse.

"See if he can expedite a restraining order," Colton suggested.

"It won't stop Devon."

"Then see if your uncle can get a squad car out there to keep watch over her."

Jessie had basically said the same thing—a stakeout...

I nodded, pulling my cell once more from my back pocket. "Be back in a few."

It took me fifteen minutes to track down my uncle, and I brushed off his questions to get caught up with each other, jumping right into my reason for calling. He listened without interruption and agreed that watching Jessie's apartment might be a good idea. I told him about the letters, the threats Devon had been sending Jessie, and he promised me he would be in touch.

Unease caused my feet to feel antsy, a sense of needing to be near Jessie and Cassie in case something went down.

"Mind if I take off?" I asked Colton an hour before our usual quitting time.

"Not at all."

I clasped his shoulder, muttered my thanks, and turned away, my strides eating up the distance to my truck.

"Call me if you need anything," Colton hollered after me.

I gave him a thumbs-up over my shoulder.

Heat trapped in the cab blasted me when I opened the door, but I hopped right in and put the windows down. Sweat trickled down my spine regardless of the rushing wind as I sped up Route 1.

A quick order to Siri for her to make a call, and I cranked the AC, put the windows up, and waited for Jessie to answer. She picked up after the fifth ring, right as my stomach started to churn.

"Hi."

A rushed exhale deflated my lungs. "You okay?"

"Yeah. Just watching TV with Cassie."

"Have you eaten anything today?"

"A piece of toast."

I pushed her to get more food into her stomach, then told her about my uncle and possibly getting a squad car on site until Devon was found. The relief in her voice made me feel the slightest bit better. She agreed to eat something more, and we hung up a few minutes later with my promise to text her later.

While I wanted to push Jessie into letting me into her apartment before Cassie's bedtime, because of the circumstances, I chose to honor her request to wait until her daughter slept without argument.

It would suck ass sitting in the truck until the sun went down cooling the air a bit, but I'd meant what I'd said.

There wasn't anything I wouldn't do for her and that sweet child who'd stolen my heart.

Chapter 28

Jessica

I kept an eye on my living room window overlooking the parking lot and took note of when Reid pulled into one of the visitor spots. He backed in to better keep a watch on the building. He was far enough away he wouldn't need to lean forward to see my second-floor window but close enough I could easily make out his face.

He lifted a hand in greeting, and the flutters in my belly brought a smile to my lips, the first of the day. I waved before turning toward Cassie who sat in her booster at the kitchen table eating generic mac and cheese.

My cell dinged, but it took me a few minutes to clean up my daughter from her early dinner. Treating her almost like a dog earlier in the afternoon, I'd worn down her energy level by playing fetch throughout the entire apartment.

In innocence, she'd scampered around, squealing and jumping like a rabbit rather than the puppy we'd decided she could be for that bit of playtime. She'd asked about her goggie a couple of times, but I redirected her focus with other things to occupy her mind.

I hadn't been as successful with my own thoughts.

Knowing I had someone in my corner, a man who sounded like he would move heaven and earth to keep us safe, wore heavy on my defenses, a dragging weight to my reservations to stand strong and hold him at arm's length.

I'd fallen asleep almost effortlessly the night before, when if alone, I wouldn't have slept a wink.

Once I had Cassie sitting down at the coffee table with crayons and a coloring book, I checked my cell.

Reid: **Redundant, but I'm out here if you need me.**

Warmth filled me, and I shook my head at myself, wondering why the hell I wanted to keep him at bay, why part of me still insisted I couldn't trust him when he'd proven himself to me.

Devon.

My smile faded as I texted out a simple thank you for Reid's assurance of being close by.

Reid: **How's Mini-Me?**

Me: **She's coloring. I'm hoping I wore her little butt out enough today that she'll go down early for me.**

Reid: **Coloring sounds like fun.**

I huffed a small laugh, able to imagine the puppy dog eyes Reid would be giving me if I could see him. Choosing to ignore his indirect request to be allowed inside earlier than agreed upon, I texted the news that Cassie had used the big girl potty three times that day.

I settled onto the couch before Reid texted back.

Reid: **You must think she's getting too big too quick. My sisters always say that about their kids.**

Me: **I've told her to slow down the growing thing, but she always tells me no way.**

Reid: **I'm not surprised.**

We chatted by text off and on over the next couple of hours, but he rang a few minutes before I decided to put a freshly-bathed Cassie to bed.

"Hey," he said by way of greeting. "My uncle just called. They're going to have a car out here in the morning."

Relief rushed through me, stinging my eyes with tears, and I recognized what I'd been ignoring since he'd left us earlier in the morning. "Thank you, Reid. I seriously don't know what I'd do without you," I told him the truth.

"You won't ever *have* to do without me if you don't want to."

Sweet butterflies once more woke in me, but I wasn't sure how to reply.

"I'm going to go grab a roast beef from that place on the corner. Do you want anything?"

He hadn't eaten dinner.

I suddenly felt like shit for making him stay outside when I could have offered him...what? Ramen? Tomato soup? Peanut butter and jelly?

"No thanks," I answered quietly. "Cassie seems ready for bed, so I'm going to put her down."

"I'll see you soon." I could hear the smile in Reid's voice, and his happiness caused warm fuzzies to swirl around like dandelion seeds on a gentle breeze through me.

Bedtime couldn't be a rushed affair, so I read Cassie's favorite book and made sure all her stuffies lined up correctly against her bed rail.

"Sleep good, baby," I whispered before kissing her forehead.

She blinked up at me with heavy eyelids, fighting the

lull of rest as always, but didn't argue when I slipped from her room, leaving the door slightly ajar.

I'd showered earlier while Cassie had sat watching her princess cartoon, so I planned on waiting in the living room for Reid to get back. Knowing he'd been a stone's throw from my apartment all evening had given me a sense of safety and peace I hadn't expected. I believed his promise to keep us safe. I was starting to believe I could entrust our hearts to him as well.

A soft knock sounded, and I bit my inner lip to stop myself from letting out a ridiculous squeal of excitement. As though my heart had been on board long before my brain got set straight, the draw to Reid proved inescapable.

Hand on the doorknob, I hesitated briefly in an attempt to still my rapidly thrumming pulse. It felt like I moved too fast in my emotions, but I admitted to myself that Reid meant more to me than Devon ever had.

My smile widened, and I threw open the door, ready to leap out and wrap my body around him.

"Devon—" His name ripped from my lungs before they squeezed like a vise, shutting off oxygen.

My ex-husband moved forward without a word, and I stumbled backward, sprawling onto the floor. Without taking his eyes off me, he quietly shut us in.

My ears rang in the silence. Adrenaline crashed through my bloodstream even as I gasped for air. Chest tight, my bladder threatening to let loose, I gaped up at him as he loomed over me.

Dreaming. I had to be. There was no way Devon had found out where I lived let alone had gotten into the building without a key code...

Reid had.

"Oh, fuck, oh, fuck," I whispered, scrambling backward from my nightmare come to life.

"No thanks," Devon sneered. "I don't stick my dick in selfish cunts who turn their back on their man at the first opportunity. See this?" He motioned at his buzzed head where thick, lush locks had always lay. "Your fault. And this?" He lifted his faded blue T-shirt, pointing at a jagged scar. "Also your fault. But the worst part of your disloyalty? I have to live in hiding for the rest of my life—so I'm going to make you pay."

I curled in on myself, cursing myself for opening the door without checking on who waited beyond first. I lamented the fact I'd left my cell on the coffee table in the living room, out of reach, useless in my greatest moment of need. But my biggest regret lay in not trusting my heart—Reid's heart—and making him wait outside when he should have shared the evening with me and Cassie.

A sense of blackness settled over my mind, a shroud of promised death. Devon would end me, I had zero doubts.

Cassie.

Rushing air slammed into my lungs, allowing oxygen to spread to my limbs. The adrenaline I so desperately needed woke me from my pitiful stupor. Devon could do whatever the fuck he wanted to me—but he wouldn't touch my daughter.

Holding his gaze, proud as *fuck* with myself for not shifting my focus off his blown pupils and face mottled by rage, I straightened. Shoulders back. Chin lifted. Hands fisted at my sides. "Leave before shit gets ugly," I told him, my voice low and wobbly.

He shifted, drawing a gun from behind his back.

I swallowed hard, eyeing the barrel mere feet from my face. "Y-You shoot that, and the p-police will be here in minutes. You'll never get out of here alive." Possible bullshit, but what other choice did I have? No silencer was attached to the gun's end, so the noise of a shot would definitely be heard by all of my surrounding neighbors.

A slow grin stretched his dried-out lips. "Guess I'll just have to use my fists then. Good thing I learned how to throw punches non-fucking-stop in that hellhole." He tucked the gun away.

I didn't see the strike that clobbered against my cheek until I hit the window and slowly slid to the floor. Dazed and ears ringing, I fought the darkness eating away at the edges of my eyesight creeping inward to steal my consciousness.

Cassie needed me—nothing, no amount of throbbing pain welling up in my face—would stop me from keeping her safe.

Trembling, I pushed upright, gritting my teeth against the desire to cry and beg for my life.

"That all you have?" I rasped, hands clenching at my sides once more to hide my shaking.

"Oh, baby doll." Devon tsked, his old pet name for me making bile rise up my throat. "I'm *so* glad to see your independent streak hasn't faded. This is going to be so much fucking fun." Wildness lit in his eyes, and I braced myself for sure death.

But he would go with me. One way or another, Devon's last breath would only draw at my mercy.

Chapter 29

Reid

The storm that had been threatening for over an hour hit full force as I waited for my roast beef, and I watched the downpour from their small shop's window facing Jessie's apartment building two blocks up the road.

I knew it would take a good twenty minutes for Jessie to get Cassie in bed, so I didn't mind the extra bit of time it took for my order number to be called while I kept an eye focused her way.

"Number seventy-six?" the girl at the counter stated loudly.

Turning from the window, I moved back toward the counter. "Thanks," I said and headed for the door and my truck I'd left idling by the curb.

There was no escaping getting soaked, so I sprinted out into the rain, hopping into my cab as quickly as possible.

"Fuck," I muttered, setting my dinner on the passenger seat before buckling up for the short ride. T-shirt soaked and work pants damp, I grimaced, hoping I wouldn't have to sit in the wet clothes for very long.

My parking spot I'd been in all afternoon still sat empty, so I backed in and cut my headlights, my windshield wipers on full force. They worked hard, barely allowing me a second of clear sight before rivulets of water blurred my vision again.

I grabbed my sandwich and tore into the fucking thing, ravenous as hell. One-handed, I shot off a text to Jessie to let her know I was back.

Half of my sandwich disappeared, and she still hadn't replied. It had been a half-hour since our last exchange when she said she was putting Cassie to bed. Maybe the little stinker was giving her problems.

Smirking at the thought of the cute kid, I tore into my sandwich, thankful the rain slapping my truck's roof had begun to lessen.

Sandwich to my mouth for another massive bite, I glanced up through the windshield freshly freed from rain by a wiper swipe.

Jessie's curtain rod and drapes hung askew.

"Fuck!"

A punch of something harsh, cold, slammed into my stomach, and I tossed my dinner onto the passenger seat. I took off through the rain, uncaring my truck still ran, its door wide open. My feet slammed onto the pavement, arms pumped, every sprinted stride across the parking lot seeming slower than nightmares when I'd tried to outrun the boogieman.

Maybe Cassie had been playing with the curtains after I'd left. Maybe Jessie had watched me drive off and had accidentally pulled it down while turning away.

"Please—fucking *Christ* don't let it be him! Fuck!" I stumbled up the entry stairs, my fingers shaking as I punched in Jessie's four-digit code.

The damn contraption beeped red at me.

"Goddamnit!" I tried again, hunkered over the fucking thing and growling like a werewolf.

Red blipped once more.

"Green you motherfucker!" I pounded in the four digits, unable to help myself—knowing I could very well break the damn box.

Green!

I yanked the door open and headed for the stairs, adrenaline like a live wire of energy zapping into every cell of my body. I started hollering Jessie's name while sprinting up the stairs two at a time.

"Jessie!" I spun around the corner, grabbing hold of the wall to keep upright. The hallway sat empty, but that didn't mean jack shit. I went for her door handle, but it didn't turn beneath my grip. I pounded on the wood, the hard thumps echoing in the stillness around me. "Jessie!"

A muffled shriek from inside hit my ears.

Curses shot through my head, but my lips stayed pressed thin, teeth clenched.

I stepped back and, putting all two-hundred and thirty pounds of myself behind my work boot, kicked at the cheap door. It tore off the top hinge but clung at the bottom.

Another cry from inside twisted my stomach, and I kicked out again, flattening the fucking thing keeping me from my girls.

Zero trace of self-preservation resided in my head. I ran through the kitchen without any thought other than to get to Jessie.

I hit the living room entrance—and pulled up short, my breath ripping from my lungs.

Jessie stood on the other side of the couch, wide-eyed

and hands clutching the arm wrapped around her neck. A handgun was pressed to her temple.

Fear should have crippled me, pushed me to my knees to beg him to let her go. Red-hot rage flared to life inside my chest like a solar flare instead, reaching out, screaming to incinerate everything in its path.

I lifted my gaze to the asshole behind her shoulder. His death wish was about to come true.

His bloodshot green eyes bore into me, and I sneered right back.

I would tear the fucker limb from limb.

"Let her go, Devon," I stated through gritted teeth.

He snorted out a sarcastic laugh. "The fuck I will."

Cassie's whimpers from her bedroom filtered through the pulse pounding in my head. "Hurt either of them and your life is over," I promised.

"Who the fuck do you think you are?" Devon waved his gun at me and yanked Jessie tighter against his chest. She kept her fear-widened eyes on my face the entire time. "You're nothing but her latest fuck buddy. She'll tire of you and toss you out with the morning trash just like she did with me."

"Mah!" Cassie cried out, the sound twisting my stomach and pulling Jessie's focus off my face. Tears welled in Jessie's eyes as a whimper escaped her trembling lips.

I held my hands up, hoping Devon would take the hint. "Let her go, man. Do it, and I won't stop you from walking out of here. I won't even call the cops."

"I wasn't born yesterday, you stupid fuck," he spat.

"Everyone all right in there?" a male voice asked from behind me.

I glanced into the kitchen to find an older gentleman in the doorway and out of sight from the living room, eyeing my boot's handiwork. "Go back to your apartment. Lock the door." *Call the cops*, I wanted to say.

He glanced up at my hands that I still held high in the air, dipped his head, and lifted a hand up to his ear like he held a phone to let me know he'd do exactly what I needed him to do.

I turned back around as Cassie cried for her mother again. Sending up a prayer Jessie's daughter wouldn't decide to get out of her bed by herself for the first time in the next few minutes, I focused my gaze on her mommy. The skin around Jessie's left eye had begun to bruise in stark contrast to the paleness of her face.

A deep growl sounded in my chest as I fought to stay put.

The hand holding the gun shook, as though Devon had rediscovered his vice that had led to his imprisonment and needed another fix.

A lit fuse, I realized, peering once more into his hazed-over eyes.

And I was going to kill him.

"Mah!" Little feet thumped on the floor and hurried down the hallway.

Shit.

In my periphery, Cassie rounded the corner. Devon's head jerked toward her, hand and gun unsteadily tipping upward.

I launched forward and dove over the couch.

Jessie wrenched herself away at the same time Devon's attention whipped back my way. He started to point the gun in my direction, but I barreled into him, and we slammed against the wall.

"Get her out of here!" I hollered at Jessie while grabbing

Devon's wrist and squeezing with every ounce of strength I had.

The fucker was ripped from prison life dumbbells, but I outweighed him—and I'd been swinging a hammer for years. He tried kneeing me in the groin, but I twisted my body and threw him to the floor.

I followed him down.

Kept a tight hold on his wrist.

Smashed his hand with the gun on the hardwood beneath us.

Devon bellowed and clocked me in the temple with his free hand, and my grip on him loosened. Motherfucker had one hell of a hook and left my ears ringing.

I returned the gesture but with less accuracy, my fist glancing off the side of his head.

He attempted a headbutt, cursing when he missed.

I jammed my knee toward his groin, his writhing making me catch him in the thigh instead.

Within seconds of our grappling, I recognized the fact I would never overpower him. More fists flew as the vision of Jessie and Cassie eating ice cream by the ocean flitted through my mind.

Devon could *not* get the upper hand—I wouldn't let him beat me.

Growling, he twisted our clasped arms, managing to pull the gun in closer. "Gonna end you." Devon sounded like a crazed lunatic, spittle flying from his lips. "Then the cheating bitch, then the brat she spawned from her unfaithful cunt!"

"No!" I hollered, even as his strength proved superior, slowly pulling the gun closer to our torsos.

The barrel wedged between our chests regardless of my rage, my determination to stop him.

Another flash of Cassie reaching for me to hold her on my shoulders ripped through my memory.

No.

I bent back his hand with all I had, desperation atop adrenaline searing through my blood.

An explosion of sound blasted, and I blinked in the sudden stillness, the sharp bite of gun smoke wafting past my nose.

"Reid!" Jessie shrieked from somewhere behind me, but all I could do was stare at the bloodshot eyes inches from my own.

I lay atop Devon, scrambling to take stock of myself, searching for pain from being shot—and feeling nothing.

Like an ice cube dropped on hot tar in summer, Devon's hold on me melted, his body going lax beneath me.

"Stay back there, Jessie! I'm fine!" I croaked.

Devon stared up at me and coughed, blood and spittle hitting me in the face.

Scrambling off him, I grabbed the gun from his limp hand, stood far enough away he couldn't kick out at me, and trained the pistol at his head.

Whimpering from both my girls became recognizable through the rushing pulse in my ears, and a sudden rush of relief coursed through me, weakening my knees.

My girls. *Mine.*

Breathe your last, fucker.

Teeth gritted, I stared down at Devon. He clutched at his chest, the stain of blood spreading on his grungy shirt widening with every gasped inhale. Wetness coated his exhales, the seconds seeming like hours as he fought for breath.

I wanted him to die. Wished for it. Fucking prayed to Mom's favorite saints no police or EMTs would arrive in time to save his sorry ass. I didn't want Jessie's nightmare to continue. Didn't need the threat of him getting his hands on her again to hinder her ability to move on.

With me.

I considered putting another bullet in the asshole's body. His brain. That would remove the chance of him ever bothering Jessie again. Without further thought, I slid my finger onto the trigger, ready and fully willing to end a man's life for the girls I loved.

A wet gurgle escaped his mouth as his gasping chest sank inward.

I waited.

He didn't inhale.

Tension kept my shoulders hitched, but the gun in my outstretched hands shook as the adrenaline crash began.

"Jessie?" I called, my voice barely audible.

"We're okay." Tears laced her soft tone, but I couldn't tear my focus off Devon's still form.

Sirens sounded in the distance, and I slowly lowered the gun to my side.

Jessie's ex would never draw breath again. He no longer had the power to dictate her actions or future.

Turning away, I caught sight of Jessie huddled on the floor in the hallway off to my right. She clutched Cassie to her chest, her wide eyes flooded with tears.

"It's over," I murmured, and she let out a soft sob, lowering her head to kiss her daughter's hair.

From their vantage point, neither of them would be able to see the man sprawled a few feet away from me, and I planned on keeping their eyes off the outcome of Devon's attempt to carry out his revenge.

I set the gun down on the coffee table, lifted my T-shirt to rub splattered blood away, and quickly made my way over to Jessie. "Let's get out of here," I murmured, sounding a hell of a lot more together than I felt.

Adrenaline still leaked through my system, making me tremble, but I managed to draw Jessie up onto her feet. She sagged against me, Cassie pressed between us.

Keeping my back to the living room and my palms against both their heads to hold them turned into me, I led them out through the kitchen and the door I'd ruined.

Cops rushed into sight around the corner, guns raised and moving fast toward us.

I sank against the hallway's wall, pulling both Jessie and Cassie onto my lap, my arms wrapped tightly around them. "Love you both so much," I rasped through the sudden thickness in my throat. "So, so much. Never letting you go."

A shuddered exhale left my lungs, and I closed my eyes, full of thankfulness.

Chapter 30

Jessica

I cracked open an eyelid and glanced around the unfamiliar bedroom. Breathing deep, I became aware of Reid's familiar woodsy scent and Cassie's underlying lavender. Warmth cradled my back, and I blinked, waiting for reality to settle into my sleep-hazed brain.

The night before rushed through my mind, hitting my heart with a punch and waking me fully.

I gasped an inhale, tensing—until I also remembered where I lay.

Attempting to slow my breaths, I glanced over my shoulder.

Cassie snuggled against Reid who slept on his side, facing both of us.

We were alive. Safe.

And Devon would never touch me again.

I sagged into the mattress, my eyes closing as nausea kicked in past the shot of fear that had jolted me awake.

Damnit.

Sliding from the bed, I swallowed hard to keep from retching all over Reid's bedroom floor. A few, quick steps took me into his bathroom, and I shut myself in. The toilet sat waiting for my grasp, and I slid to my knees, shaking hands gripping the cool porcelain.

Breathing deeply, I willed the nausea away, focusing on the memory of Cassie and Reid clinging to each other in peaceful sleep rather than reliving the night before.

Luckily, neither Cassie nor I had caught sight of Devon in the living room, and we'd left the building before the coroner had removed his body from my apartment.

Devon is dead.

My stomach heaved, but nothing came out as I coughed over the toilet bowl.

Gone forever—we were truly safe.

I thought I'd sobbed my emotions dry the night before while Reid had held me in his arms after Cassie had passed out, but fresh tears coursed down my face.

Footsteps shuffled behind me, and a hand gathered my hair back away from my face as I retched a second time.

"You okay?" Reid asked, the warmth in his voice pouring over me, erasing the chill that had taken over me.

"Y-yeah," I whispered, eyes clenched shut. A shuddered sigh tore through me, and I sagged back onto my heels.

Reid shifted behind me, settling down onto the floor. "Come here."

He tugged, and I crawled, plastering myself against his chest, his hard thighs beneath me and the heat of his chest warming my cheek, same as when we'd hunkered in the hallway and Reid told me he loved us.

His words had been too much—but I would never be able to hear them enough. The way he'd fearlessly faced down death to protect us...

"Cassie's still sleeping," he whispered against my hair as I fought off tears of gratefulness I would never be able to fully voice. "Devon will never bother you ever again, and I love you so much. I would have gladly taken a bullet fifty times over to keep you both safe."

The tears spilled at his second declaration, but I swallowed against the sobs that would wake my daughter.

Reid held me in silence, his hands smoothing over my back and legs curled against him. Peace rested beneath my release of emotions, slowly taking over as my tears lessened. I breathed deeply, my face squashed against his skin, filling my lungs with the comforting scent of him.

"Better?" he asked, his thumbs running circles on my back.

I murmured an affirmative and sighed, snuggling even deeper into his hold. So warm. Gentle. Kind.

A shiver slid over my skin as a deep sense of thankfulness flooded through me. What would have happened if Reid hadn't seen the askew curtain and assumed the worst? And what sort of scene would have greeted the police when they were eventually called?

I imagined both me and Cassie wouldn't have been alive to see the outcome of Devon's promise to make me pay for what I'd done.

Wrapping my arms around Reid, I lifted my face off his chest.

Dark, warm eyes peered at me with so much emotion my chest ached.

"Thank you," I whispered, and tenderness filled his gaze as he brushed his thumb over my jaw.

"Anything for my girls."

My girls.

That tightness around my heart intensified, and I leaned toward him, needing his lips.

But I hesitated. "I love you too, Reid," I croaked out, my voice raspy from all the crying I'd been powerless to stop.

His slow smirk, the twinkle in his eyes, tempted me to slap his cocky ass. At least he didn't tease me.

Our mouths met with gentleness, but need for him rushed through me all the same.

Later.

Pulling away, I once more settled my cheek against his chest and soaked in the comfort he offered. "What time is it?"

Reid ran his fingers through my ratty hair. "Almost nine."

"Shit!" I tried to pull away, but he tightened his hold on me. "I never called off work!" I huffed.

"It's already taken care of. I also got in touch with Colton, letting him know I wouldn't be in today. Tomorrow too."

Exhaustion once more took over my body, and I leaned into his strength. Who needed stubborn independence when the most giving man I knew offered to keep me from physical harm and emotionally afloat?

"Come on." Reid stood and swung me up into his arms without difficulty, carrying me back into his bedroom.

Cassie let out a soft snore but didn't move from Reid's spot.

He chuckled and laid me on the opposite side. "Scoot over," he whispered and crawled in beside me. He pulled the comforter up over us and stretched out, facing me.

Grasping my waist, he tugged me closer, sliding one of his legs between mine. "I was so afraid I was going to lose the best thing I've ever found," he whispered, pushing my hair back from my face, his dark eyes intent on mine. "Thank God you messed up that curtain, otherwise I would have waited for your text telling me Cassie was sleeping. I would have been too late."

I'd thought the same thing and had fought off the image of that outcome while trying to fall asleep the night before.

Longing to forget swept over me, and I leaned in, kissing him. Needing him.

My eyes stung.

Fucking *again*.

"I want you so bad right now," he murmured against my lips, hitching my leg up around his waist. "I was afraid I was going to lose you."

I clung to him as he grasped my head, keeping him in place to ravage my mouth regardless of morning breath. Since he didn't care, neither did I. The sense of life—*living* —swelled inside me as Reid's dick thickened against my core.

He pressed, and I gyrated my hips gently, our combined efforts upping the need for release between us.

"Think we can get away with slow and silent?" he whispered, smoothing his hand from my knee up to my ass, pushing his T-shirt I'd slept in past my hips.

I hummed an agreement, quiet and stealth-like shimmying out of my panties as he slid his sweats down enough the heat of his cock pressed against me. Shirts separated the skin of our chests, but our mouths came together, my arousal kicking in fully. He caressed my spine, my ass, grinding the back of his dick against my clit.

"Need you," I whispered, reaching between us to grab his length.

Our gazes held as I shifted, notching his thick head inside me.

"Condom," he breathed the word through gritted teeth.

"It's okay."

"Yeah?"

I smiled, clasping his scruffy cheek in my hand. "Yes."

He grasped my backside and pulled me into him, filling me with one slow thrust. "Fuck," he whispered harshly, eyes rolling back into his head. "So silky and wet." Groaning quietly, he took my mouth and began rocking in and out of my body, the slow drags addictive and arousing as hell.

"Feels so good," I murmured against his lips, aware of Cassie's soft snores behind me.

Reid hummed his agreement, grinding his hips against mine. "Could stay right here forever."

"Mmm," I agreed, running my fingers into his hair to pull his mouth back to mine.

We moved in near silence, the shifting of blankets and heavy breaths the only sounds. I wanted to bathe in our lovemaking, to draw out every second, soak in every caress of his tongue, every drag of his length through my core, but I knew our time grew short.

I slid my hand between us, my fingers finding my clit.

"Yes," Reid whispered against my mouth. "Come on my dick, sweetheart."

A few, slow strokes over my hardened nub, and release slid through me, a stinging ache settling in my chest.

Reid let out a soft curse, burying his dick deep inside me, his face in my neck as I gave him what he wanted. "Jesus, Jessie."

He pulled out quickly and thrust against my belly. His dick bucked, wet heat erupting between us, sending another rush of euphoria over my skin. Moaning deeply, he took my mouth, gasping with every spurt he spilled onto my stomach.

Panting for breath, we stilled, too warm and tingling in satiated bliss.

Our gazes met, and in that moment, I recognized the fact I didn't want another day to pass without Reid in our lives. He'd weaseled his way in, and I was done fighting. I had admitted to falling in love with him, but would he be interested in an exclusive relationship going forward?

I opened my mouth to ask, but a little knee poked me in the spine.

"Mah?" a sleepy voice mumbled.

A soft smile curved Reid's lips as he shifted away from me and pulled his sweats back up over his dick.

Smirking, I quickly swiped his T-shirt down from where it had shoved up to my breasts, doing my best to wipe up the mess he'd made on me.

"Mah!" Cassie sounded fully alert, the bed jostling. "Goggie!" she shrieked, obviously having sat up and caught sight of who lay on my opposite side. She scrambled over me, sharp elbows and knees digging into my body.

"Ow!" I laughed, rolling away to escape the abuse.

Cassie landed atop Reid with a giggle.

"Welcome to my life," I muttered without a hint of annoyance. "I can't even pee in peace."

"Morning, Bossy-Boo," Reid said with a chuckle, helping her to sit on his torso.

She grasped the hair sticking up on top of his head and did a little dance, her pull-up covered bum rubbing his chest. "My goggie!"

Reid's chuckle, the pure happiness radiating from him flooded my heart with the same emotions. "Yes, I'm your doggie and always will be if your mom agrees." He glanced over at me, eyes twinkling, lady-killer smile flashing his white teeth.

I wasn't sure what all he was asking for, but I wasn't about to question. I simply answered, "Yes."

Chapter 31

Reid

I hadn't even parked in my parent's driveway, and my entire family streamed out of their house. All three sisters, their husbands, and five wild kids tumbled across the front lawn while Mom and Dad stayed up on the stoop, hands clasped between them.

"Oh boy," Jessie breathed the words like a curse, and I glanced over to find her eyes wide, pure panic lashing over her features.

Putting the car into park, I reached over and laced my fingers through hers. "They're going to love you. Promise."

She swallowed hard and glanced into the back seat.

"They'll love Cassie too."

"No way!" Cassie hollered, and I chuckled.

"Unca!" Small fists beat on the driver's door, and my grin widened at the fiasco to come.

"Ready?" I asked.

"No," Jessie said, shaking her head.

I'd begged her for two solid weeks to go to my parents for a Sunday brunch, and I'd only gained her agreement after a solid hour of climax denial the night before. Once I had her breathless, sweaty, and moaning about how much of a prick I was, Jessie was ready to promise me anything in exchange for my dick to rub her just right.

She was lucky I'd only asked her to meet my family.

I had plans for our future—but I knew she wasn't yet ready. She and Cassie had stayed with me for three days after the incident with Devon, and although she'd claimed to want her space still, she suggested I stay over at their place more often than not.

Her apartment had been professionally cleaned, the front door replaced, but I could tell memories from that night continued to haunt her mind with how her gaze flitted around the living room, every sharp, unexpected noise jolting her wherever she sat. I hoped it wouldn't take months before she agreed to just move into my condo like I'd been begging her to do. At my place, there would be no flashbacks to cause more stress. She belonged with me. Beside me. In my bed.

But she'd yet to agree for whatever reason.

"Let's do this," I said before kissing her knuckles.

Inhaling deeply, she nodded.

The second I opened my door, rug rats leaped on me, giggles and grasping hands splitting my face into a grin.

"Mah!" Cassie called from the backseat. "Ah out too! Ah play!"

Peeling the kids off me as I straightened would have proven futile, so I let them hang on my arms, two sitting on my feet and grasping my calves.

"I brought a new friend," I told my nieces and nephews, "but you have to let go of me so I can bring her out to meet you!" I laughed the statement, the little brats ignoring every single word.

Glancing over at my sisters who eyed me with pleased

smiles, I hefted my forearms up, my oldest niece clinging to the right, her two younger siblings dangling from the left. "A little help here?"

Jessie climbed from the car as my sisters moved in to relieve me of their leeches. She rounded the back and approached, pink flushing her cheeks. Even though I knew she'd been unnerved the entire ride to Malden, the soft upward curve of her lips and the light in her eyes assured me all would be well.

I unbuckled Cassie and set her onto the grass—she bolted after the parcel of kids waiting for her a few feet away, her little legs flying. "Hi!" she yelled without a care in the world. She was accepted into the fold without any fuss, and they took off as a bunch, shrieking giggles across Dad's front lawn.

I turned, reaching for Jessie's hand. She slid hers into my hold, and I squeezed. "Margo, Marie, Macey, this is Jessie," I tugged her against my side, giving her something solid to lean against. "Be kind, or I'll never talk to you again."

Margo, the oldest of my younger sisters, snorted and moved up into Jessie's personal space, pulling her out of my embrace. *Our* family's bossy-boo hugged my girl tight, welcoming her to the clan.

Once my other sisters and all three of my brothers-in-law stated the same with slight variations of wording, tears welled in Jessie's eyes.

She never expected to have another family, let alone one as large and boisterous in their acceptance as mine.

We finally were allowed to approach the house, and Mom beamed down at us, slowly descending from the stoop to greet the next woman she would eventually have the pleasure of calling daughter.

I hoped, anyway.

Jessie no longer held me at arm's length. She didn't care when I showed up at her apartment, didn't try to hide my presence in the mornings when I'd slept over. To me, that meant I was golden. Good to go.

I just had to find the right time to thoroughly put my heart on the line and tell her exactly what I wanted.

Dad was the only one to not hug the breath out of Jessie, but I'd expected it and had told Jessie he wouldn't. While the man tended toward gruff and quiet, the dark eyes I'd inherited from him gave away his true emotions. Tenderness rested in his gaze as he tracked after Cassie shrieking and playing tag with the other grandchildren in the yard.

Twinkling, those dark orbs turned toward Jessie, and he quietly welcomed her with a brief handshake.

Mom elbowed him, and Dad's cheeks flushed.

"Could they be any more adorable," Jessie whispered to me as we followed my parents into the house.

"I warned you."

And I had. About the level of noise at the two tables they tucked together with added sections so our entire family could eat together. The massive created table spanned from the dining room straight into the living area, the wall between having been ripped out the summer before to create a bigger space since our family didn't show signs of stopping its expansion anytime soon.

I told Jessie my sisters would be too busy with their kids while eating to ask her any questions, and I'd been careful to make sure Mom sat Jessie beside her with Cassie in between us. Luckily, the extra child on hand had proven enough excitement to keep the others wound up, demanding their moms' attention.

Dad asked about Jessie's work, talking to her about their

bundled insurance policies, and her smile when promising to give him a quote warmed my chest.

I bent over and whispered into Cassie's ear to look at how pretty her mommy was. Cassie didn't verbally respond but beamed up at Jessie, leaned over, and kissed her arm.

And goddamn, how that warmth expanded, settling into a sweet ache in my heart.

I loved Jessie. Loved Cassie. No doubt about it, the emotions I felt for both of them had grown ten times more potent than what I'd had with Tara.

Dessert in the form of an upside-down pineapple cake arrived in Marie's hands, Macey bringing up the rear with a tub of homemade ice cream.

"You weren't kidding," Jessie mumbled at me after a few bites of each. "These are heavenly."

"I know how to make both," I claimed, waggling my eyebrows.

She rolled her eyes but didn't bother hiding her grin.

Perhaps the rest of the way into Jessie's heart would be through her stomach. Considering how she'd put away Mom's meatloaf and mashed potatoes—both recipes having been perfected with my help years earlier—I expected I would leap over whatever final hurdle she still held strong between us that made her slow on the decision to move in with me.

Whatever it was, it was going down.

Chapter 32

Jessica

To say Reid's family was overwhelming would be an understatement, but the easy acceptance of an outsider into their bubble of happiness filled me with wonder.

They also scared the shit out of me with their knowing glances and his sisters' winks at me whenever Reid pressed a kiss to my temple or slipped his hand around my waist. I didn't doubt they expected forever between the two of us, and while I longed for the same, I feared Reid would eventually grow bored with one woman, one pussy, for the rest of his life.

He'd been an escort—his family had even known and not cared about his chosen profession earlier in the year.

Seriously, who were these people?

Shaking my head I watched him carry Cassie into my apartment building and up the stairs ahead of me. She'd played herself out with all the Sullivan's grandchildren, sleeping heavily, mouth hanging open within minutes of being buckled into her car seat for the ride home.

Maybe it would be the eventual burden he felt from a ready-made family that would send him packing…

Pushing against the nagging thoughts that always prodded me to guard myself, I unlocked my door and stepped back, letting Reid take the lead.

Tucked against his chest, my sweet girl remained clueless about any harsh realities, the choices I'd made, and those still ahead of me. But one thing I knew for sure after only a few handful of hours with Reid's family.

I wanted to *try* for forever. Screw self-preservation and what-ifs. Taking the risk would be worth all I stood to gain as Reid had shown since day one.

Uninhibited affection. Words of edification. Help in raising my daughter. Someone to lean on when shit got real. A man to hold me when I grew tired of being strong, which had been too often the previous few months.

"Can I take her into her bed?" Reid asked, and I put my purse and keys onto the kitchen table.

I turned to face him in the silence, drinking in the sight of him and Cassie together. Reid stood so tall and handsome, his wide shoulders and strong arms gladly bearing the weight of the precious gift I loved more than anything in the world.

I prayed he never grew tired of her, that she would burrow even deeper into his heart than he claimed she already had, never to be plucked out.

"Yes," I whispered but with more meaning than the simple answer he'd asked for.

As though hearing and understanding what I agreed to, Reid smiled even as his eyes darkened. A slow smirk lifted one corner of his mouth. "Yeah?"

"Yes," I repeated, my chin lifting, reminding him of my

stubbornness to get shit done and see things through. But this time, he would be beside me.

Keeping his focus on my face, Reid lowered his head and kissed the top of Cassie's. "Go ready yourself for me, sweetheart," he whispered, his quiet voice filled with desire.

My breath left in a rush as arousal hit me hard in the belly. Knees instantly weak, I watched him take Cassie back down the hallway.

He'd asked to put her to bed, something I'd never allowed anyone but me to do before. Surely he knew I wanted more with him, that I trusted him with my daughter.

After a quick trip to the bathroom to take care of business and brush my teeth, I ambled across the hallway into my still-empty bedroom. I turned on the monitor before stripping down, listening as Reid read Goodnight Moon even though Cassie probably already snored. God, the ache rushing through my chest filled me with the most addictive, delicious pain.

Crawling under the sheets in nothing but my skin, I waited, my heart beating heavy in my chest.

Nighttime hadn't fully fallen, but it had been a long day, and even if Reid hadn't suggested the bedroom, I'd have gone there on my own.

Reid smiled when catching sight of me in bed. Gaze glued to my face, he quietly shut the door behind him. Normally, he outright questioned if he could stay the night, but he'd *heard* me earlier in the kitchen and knew I no longer wanted him to ask.

He pulled his shirt off overhead, revealing his tanned, muscle-lined torso.

My mouth watered, my gaze latching onto his hands as he unzipped his jeans. His fingers lingered along the open waist, thumbs rubbing over his happy trail to the root of his dick.

A humph of annoyance flitted past my lips, and he chuckled, shoving down his jeans and boxer briefs with one push.

Half-hard, his dick hung heavy between his thick thighs. He grasped his base and slid his hand upward, tugging as my pulse picked up its pace. "Want it?"

"You know I do." I didn't bother trying to hide the heavy desire I felt coursing through me from my voice.

Reid climbed onto the bed and ripped the sheet off me, growling his appreciation at seeing my lack of clothing. He crawled over me on all fours, his eyes seeming to drink in my heated face, parted lips, and needy gaze.

Lowering his body, he rested his warm weight atop me from chest to toes, his larger thighs bracketing mine to keep my legs tightly together. His hard length pressed against the seam of my thighs, and elbows on the mattress, he planked, our mouths inches apart.

A sweet hint of vanilla from a second helping of home-made ice cream laced his breath, and I filled my lungs while winding my fingers into his hair, waiting to see if he would get straight to the action or explain why he peered at me as though trying to figure something out.

The silence stretched as we shared breath, and I couldn't look away from the intensity in his dark eyes.

"What are you thinking, Reid?" I finally asked, wanting his mind at rest so we could get on to the good stuff.

"I know it's really soon," he said, studying my eyes, "but fuck it. I want you in my life. Every sunrise. Every night. I want to watch cartoons in the morning with your precious daughter. Want you wrapped around my body while the stars shine. Want to drink in your laughter at dinner time.

Hear about your day. Enjoy Cassie as she grows up. I want to be the father that little girl deserves, the man who will show her what true love looks like."

His words hit me harder than Devon's fists had that night, ripping the air from my lungs, but the pain felt different. This wasn't another plea for us to move in with him, but a desire for more. A future together—the three of us.

A swelling need to say yes once more rose inside me, but I couldn't find my voice.

Reid thumbed over my lips, but his gaze lingered on my eyes. "I was always jealous of my sisters with their kids. I want some of my own one day, but for right now, a ready-made family is nothing short of perfect. I couldn't ask for a better third wheel situation."

I bit back my smile, hating how easily he swayed me to give in to his dreams. Imagining carrying Reid's baby in my belly, watching Cassie cradle her younger sibling in her small arms for the first time...

Yes, I wanted that. So badly.

Tugging Reid's head down, I brushed my lips over his, butterflies erupting inside me as always from his kiss.

"Let's date," I whispered against his mouth. "Live together like you've been begging for, get to know each other. I want to make sure Cassie doesn't drive you insane before we start making life-altering decisions like adding more kids to the mix."

"But we can practice?" he asked, shifting to weasel his legs then hips between mine.

Lifting my knees, I wrapped my ankles around his ass and clutched him close. The head of his dick rested at my opening, and even though I liked to be in control, I loved that he held the upper hand in deciding when and how he would fill me.

"Practice makes perfect," he murmured with an enticing tone, swiveling his hips enough that he breached my opening.

"You're already that and so much more." I lifted my head to take his mouth, and he slid into me with one slow glide.

My body stretched to accommodate his girth as though welcoming him home.

Reid felt like that to me. My place of comfort and rest. Safety.

Clasped tightly together, we kissed, our bodies one, our hearts sharing time and space in a moment I would never forget.

Had he asked again while I drowned in passion beneath him, I would have agreed to be his wife without hesitation. Carry those babies he wanted. Grow old and feeble alongside him. Watch our children become adults and create their own happily ever afters, gifting us with prolonged joy at what love could produce.

Yes, I loved Reid. Somehow, some way, he'd found a way through my walls, and I couldn't be happier he'd persevered.

Chapter 33

Reid

Four Months Later...

Jessie ran from the breakfast table to the bathroom for the third morning in a row, her robe flapping behind her. I glanced down at Cassie who had climbed onto my lap a few seconds earlier after deciding she didn't want any more of her breakfast. "Mommy's not feeling good again," I told my little munchkin.

Her blonde eyebrows furrowed as she turned toward where her mother had escaped the scent of toast and coffee. "Canny?"

"Candy?"

She nodded, her eyes wide with concern, probably remembering how she'd eaten too many Skittles on Halloween. We'd been with my family in Malden that cold night, all the grandkids like a pack of banshees running from house to house while the parents, me, Mom, and Dad had tagged along behind, taking countless pictures and making what I hoped would be the first of many memories to come of my favorite holiday.

"You think too much candy made mommy's belly hurt?"

I asked for clarity, shifting Cassie into my left arm so I could reach my mug.

She nodded again, pressing against my chest—her favorite place to rest on the rare moments outside of watching TV. Otherwise? The girl was a whirlwind of energy, keeping me on my toes to find ways to snag her attention and wear her little ass out so she'd crash at night and I could love on her mommy without the worry of being interrupted.

I smiled and ruffled the mess of blonde hair knotted from sleep in her new big girl bed I'd set up the day before in what used to be my guest room. It had been painted—purple—with a Mimimus, the pink pig, and Princess Sophia mural created by my sister Macey, the only artist in the family.

"Pretty sure it isn't candy," I told Cassie.

I hoped it wasn't, anyway. Jessie took precautions, but the pill wasn't one hundred percent effective. Giddiness rose up inside me, and I fought off the need to shift, the same as Cassie always did unless snuggling against me or zoned out with her cartoons. She moved around, her little bum too bony for how plump she was.

"Sit still, wiggle butts, and finish your toast."

She complied, chewing the piece I'd handed her, her gaze flitting toward the hallway a few times.

"Mommy's going to be just fine," I assured her, kissing the rat's nest atop her head.

"Ugh." Jessie stumbled back into the kitchen a minute later, the back of her hand pressed to her mouth. Her worn flower robe she refused to get rid of hung askew over her chest, allowing me an eyeful of rounded breast just shy of a nipple. She scowled, but I'd never seen anything so damn beautiful in my life. "What the hell is *wrong* with me?" she grumbled. "I can't kick this bug!"

I chuckled and pushed her chair out again with my foot beneath the table, pretty damn sure I'd figured out what the issue was.

"It's not funny!" she insisted with a pout I wanted to kiss off her luscious mouth.

Growing up with three sisters, I'd become a master at knowing when to hide away from emotional basket cases. At least two months had passed since Jessie had curled up in bed with chocolate and a heating pad, telling me to give her three feet—or *rub* her feet.

"Where are you in your cycle?" I asked, still grinning like a fool.

Her face scrunched up as she plopped back down on her chair and pushed her plate of a half-eaten bagel off to the side. She hadn't even finished her first cup of coffee. "I-I'm not sure. Between everything that happened, moving in with you, and Christine's dad buying another book of business last month—" Her gaze jerked my way, her pale face taking on a sickly pallor. "Oh, *shit*," she breathed, her eyes widening.

"No-no word, Mah!" Cassie said, and I squeezed her just a little tighter.

"Well?" I pushed, not the least bit offended by Jessie's look of horror. We wanted kids together, but I had agreed to date her and settle in for at least a year before making any further decisions because it was what she wanted.

"I think I skipped last month," she whispered.

"You sure?" I was—and I was also *very* sure I wanted things to change in our lives a lot faster than she had hoped for.

She bit her lip and moaned, her eyes filling with tears.

Fuck. What was it about Jessie and Cassie's matching orbs welling with wetness that punched me straight in the chest? Their tears also roused all my protectiveness and the need to lavish whatever they needed on them. Hugs and kisses were my favorite, but quiet words of assurance of how far I would go to make them both happy were a close second.

Because there wasn't anything I wouldn't do for my girls. Absolutely nothing.

I slid my chair farther back from the table to make more room and held out my hand. "Get over here," I said, beckoning with my outstretched fingers.

As always when overwhelmed, Jessie took a few seconds to try to figure out the tumbling shit inside on her own, and I waited patiently, knowing she would eventually comply and let me shoulder whatever emotional burden she carried. I craved being there for her every need, and the previous couple of months had proven she did too.

But I let her have her time of independence. She would recognize accepting help didn't make her any less strong, the same as she always did.

With a heavy sigh, she finally gave in to my request, allowing her stubbornness to take a back seat so I could offer comfort and support.

I tugged her down onto my right thigh and kissed her good and hard until she sagged against my chest like her daughter did from her perch on my other side.

Cassie giggled. "Kisses!"

I tore my mouth off Jessie, the purest, sweetest happiness welling up inside me at having both of my girls in my arms. "The best," I told my little munchkin before smooching her button nose with loud smacks of my lips. "You know, Bossy-Boo, I think my days of being the third wheel in this relationship are officially over. We're going to be a full-on four-wheel drive in eight months or so. What do you think of that?"

"No way!"

I snorted with laughter, and the wiggle butt slid off my lap, streaking straight for the living room.

"Ah, Phia!" she hollered.

"That's not how we ask for things!" I called back.

I heard her humph of annoyance through the wall separating us.

Glancing back over at the love of my life, I knew the answer I'd been wanting from her lips would be different from the other half-dozen times I'd attempted to talk her into relenting to the certain future I saw for us.

A tear slid down Jessie's cheek, and I swiped it away with my thumb. "I'm getting tired of asking, Jessica Lindy, but *now* will you marry me?"

She laughed as more tears rolled. "Ye—"

I kissed the word off her lips as Cassie loudly whined, "*Pease*" in a sweet, begging tone I knew I would give in to forever.

THE END

About the Author

USA Today bestselling author Lynn Burke is a CrossFit and coffee addict. Her three spawn and two fur babies dictate how often she can be found hunched over her Mac, typing as fast as her fickle muse cooks up hot stories.

You can find more about Lynn at her website: www.authorlynnburke.com

Also By Lynn Burke

Abel's Obsession

Divulging Secrets

Healing Storms

In Between

Reluctant Lumberjack

Resisting his Mate

Billion Dollar Love Anthology

Blood Born Series

Bonds of Worship Series

Dark Leopards MC

Darkest Desires Series

Devil's Outlaws MC

Elite Escort Series

Elite Escorts MM Series

Fallen Gliders MC

Forbidden Obsession Duet

Found by Fate Series

Midnight Sun Series

Missing Link Series

Risso Family Series

Sandy Ridge Series

Sinful Nature Series

Vicious Vipers MC

www.ingramcontent.com/pod-product-compliance
Lightning Source LLC
Chambersburg PA
CBHW070500200726
48293CB00007B/2303